QUESTIONS

DID YOU MAKE UP YOUR BED?

YEAH. CAN YOU PUT BANANAS IN MY PANCAKES, PLEASE?

DID YOU FINISH YOUR HOMEWORK?

YEAH. CAN WE PLAY A QUICK GAME OF PING-PONG, MOM?

AND WHAT ABOUT THE READING. I DIDN'T SEE YOU DOING THAT YESTERDAY.

MOM, DAD'S NOT EVEN HERE.

JUST BECAUSE YOUR FATHER'S AWAY DOESN'T MEAN YOU CAN AVOID YOUR CHORES.

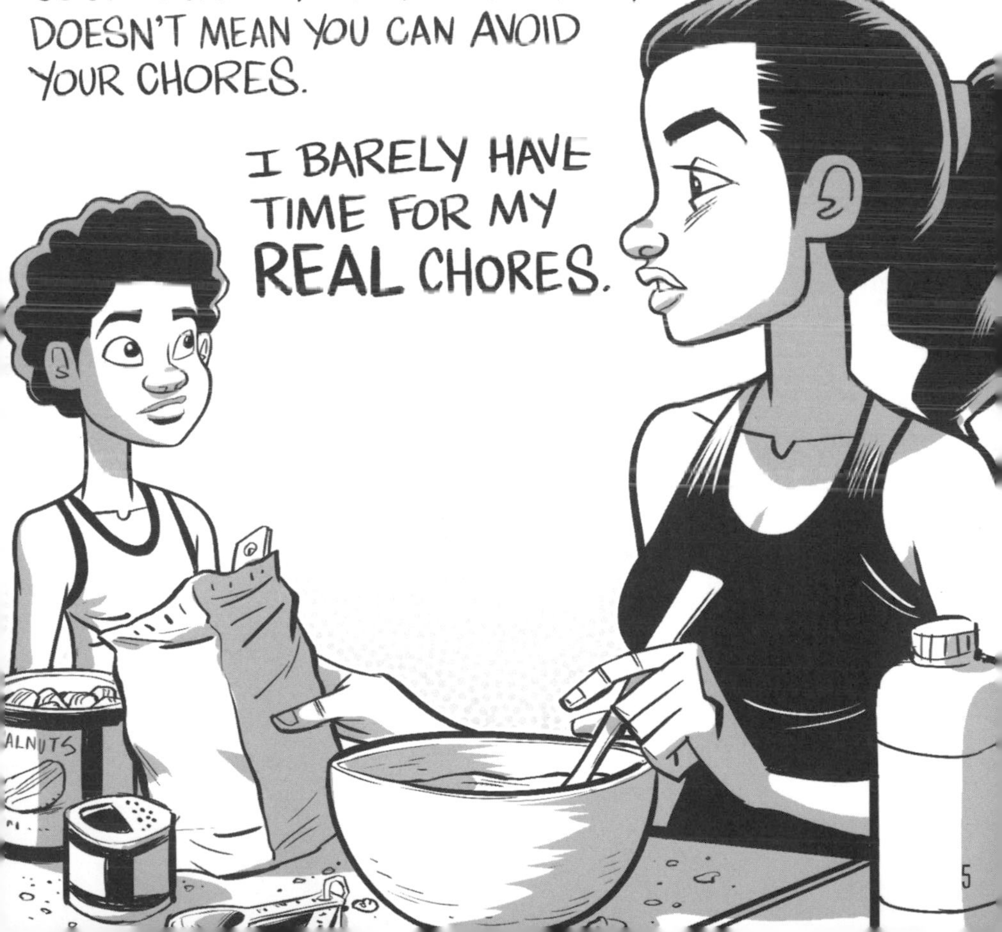
I BARELY HAVE TIME FOR MY **REAL** CHORES.
ALNUTS

PERHAPS YOU SHOULD SPEND LESS TIME PLAYING **XBOX** AT ALL HOURS OF THE NIGHT.

HUH?

OH, YOU THINK I DIDN'T KNOW?

I'M SICK OF READING HIS STUPID WORDS, MOM. I'M GOING TO HIGH SCHOOL NEXT YEAR AND I SHOULDN'T HAVE TO KEEP DOING THIS.

WHY COULDN'T YOUR DAD

BE A MUSICIAN LIKE JIMMY LEON'S DAD OR OWN AN OIL COMPANY LIKE COBY'S?

BETTER YET, WHY COULDN'T HE BE A COOL DETECTIVE DRIVING A SLEEK SILVER CONVERTIBLE CAR LIKE **WILL SMITH** IN **BAD BOYS?**

INSTEAD, YOUR DAD'S A LINGUISTICS PROFESSOR WITH CHRONIC **VERBOMANIA*** AS EVIDENCED BY THE FACT THAT HE ACTUALLY WROTE A DICTIONARY CALLED **WEIRD** AND **WONDERFUL WORDS** WITH, **GET THIS,** FOOTNOTES.

*VERBOMANIA [VURB-OH-MEY-NEE-UH]
NOUN: A CRAZED OBSESSION FOR WORDS. EVERY FREAKIN' DAY I HAVE TO READ HIS "DICTIONARY," WHICH HAS FREAKIN' FOOTNOTES. THAT'S ABSURD TO ME. KINDA LIKE ORDERING A GLASS OF CHOCOLATE MILK, THEN ASKING FOR CHOCOLATE SYRUP ON THE SIDE. SERIOUSLY, WHO DOES THAT? SMH!

7

IN THE ELEMENTARY SCHOOL SPELLING BEE

WHEN YOU INTENTIONALLY MISSPELLED **HEIFER**, HE ALMOST HAD A **COW**.

YOU'RE THE ONLY KID ON YOUR BLOCK AT SCHOOL IN **THE. ENTIRE. FREAKIN. WORLD.**

WHO LIVES IN A

PRISON OF WORDS

HE CALLS IT THE PURSUIT OF EXCELLENCE.

YOU CALL IT

SHAWSHANK.

AND EVEN THOUGH YOUR MOTHER FORBIDS YOU TO SAY IT, THE TRUTH IS

YOU HATE WORDS!

GIDDY-UP

SHE HOLLERS, **SMASHING** THE BALL TO THE EDGE OF THE RIGHT CORNER OF THE TABLE WITH S MUCH FORCE,

IT SENDS YOU DIVING INTO THE LAUNDRY STACK, TRYING AND FAILING TO LOB IT **BACK**.

LOSER DOES THE DISHES TONIGHT. YOU CAN'T SAY THAT NOW, MOM. IT'S GAME POINT.

SHE DROPS A SHOT
RIGHT OVER THE NET
THAT YOU CAN'T GET TO.

YOU'RE A **ONE-TRICK PONY,**
YOUNG BOY.

STICK TO SOCCER,
SHE JOKES, THEN
HEADLOCKS YOU,
HITS YOU ON THE
BACKSIDE WITH HER
PADDLE, AND SOAKS
YOUR FOREHEAD IN
KISSES AFTER BEATING
YOU FOR THE **FOURTH**
GAME IN A ROW.

11

Mom

USED TO RACE HORSES, BUT NOW SHE ONLY TRAINS THEM.

CORRECTION: SHE **USED TO** TRAIN THEM, WHICH WAS PRETTY **AWESOME**, ESPECIALLY WHEN YOU GOT TO COWBOY AROUND THE NEIGHBORHOOD OR WATCH THE **PREAKNESS** FROM LUXURY BOX SEATS WITH **UNLIMITED COKE** AND **SHRIMP.**

BUT SHE DOESN'T DO IT ANYMORE SINCE THERE ARE NO **HORSES** IN THE **CITY.**

LAST YEAR, SHE DID GET ASKED TO TRAIN A HORSE NAMED **BITE MY DUST,** BUT WHEN SHE REVEALED THAT WE'D HAVE TO MOVE TO SOME SMALL TOWN WITH NO UNIVERSITY (OR TRAVEL SOCCER TEAM), DAD SAID **NO** WITH A CAPITAL **N.**

BLACKJACK ON THE WAY TO SCHOOL

WITH TWO SEVENS SHOWING,
YOU SAY, HIT ME!
COBY CURSES WHEN
YOU GET A THIRD.

BLACK JACK!

MS. HARDWICK'S HONORS ENGLISH CLASS
IS ONE BORING REQUIRED READ AFTER ANOTHER.
SO YOU'VE BECOME A PRO AT DAYDREAMING WHILE
PRETEND-LISTENING.

THE BEAUTIFUL GAME

YOU'RE **PUMPED.** THE MATCH IS TIED AT THE END OF EXTRA TIME.

PLAYERS GATHER AT CENTER CIRCLE FOR THE COIN TOSS.

YOU CALL TAILS AND **WIN.**

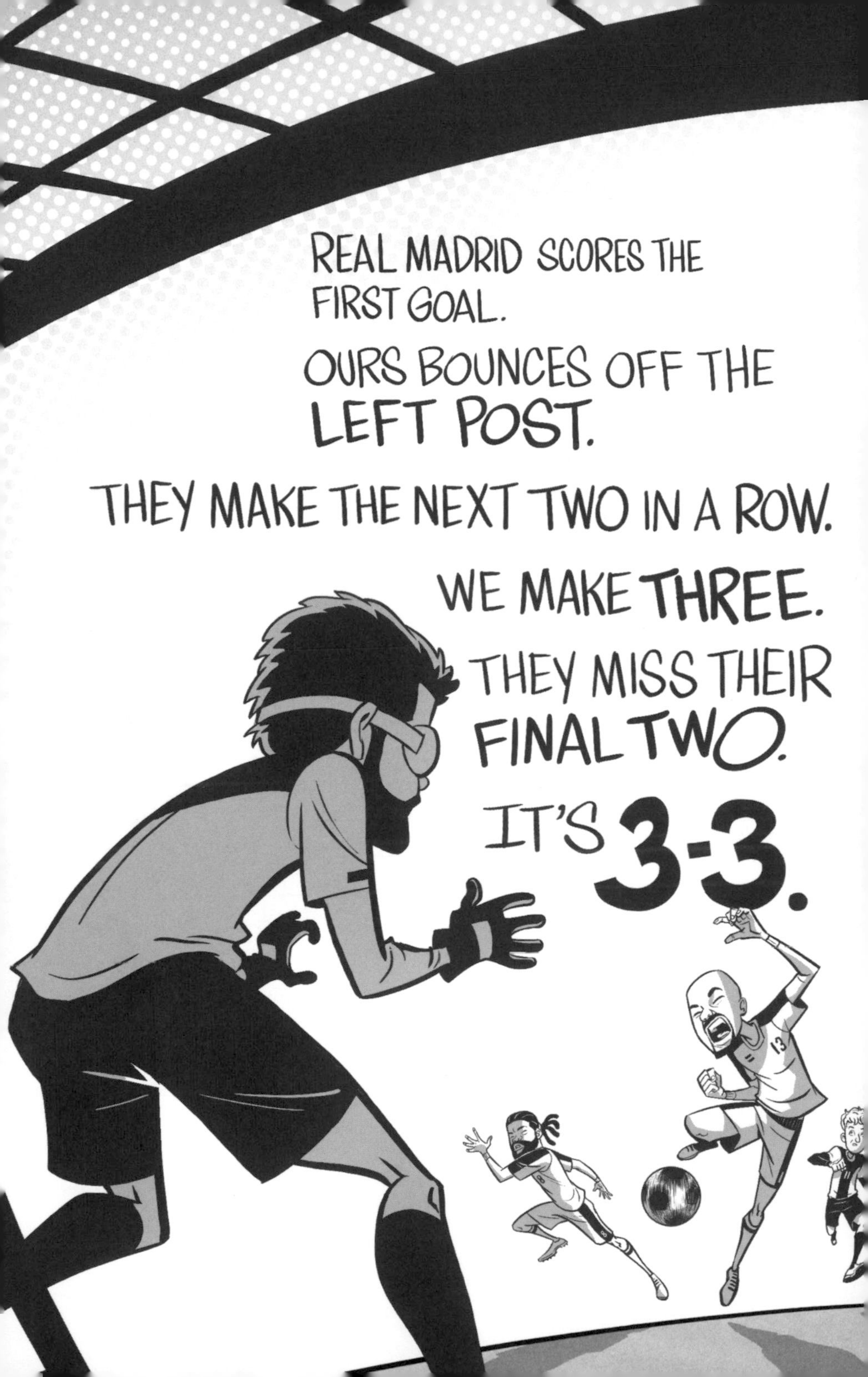
REAL MADRID SCORES THE FIRST GOAL.
OURS BOUNCES OFF THE LEFT POST.
THEY MAKE THE NEXT TWO IN A ROW.
WE MAKE THREE.
THEY MISS THEIR FINAL TWO.
IT'S 3-3.

YOUR TURN TO **REV** THE **ENGINE**,
TURN ON THE **JETS**.

SCORE, AND YOU WIN

TEAMMATES LOCK ARMS
FOR THE **FINAL KICK**.

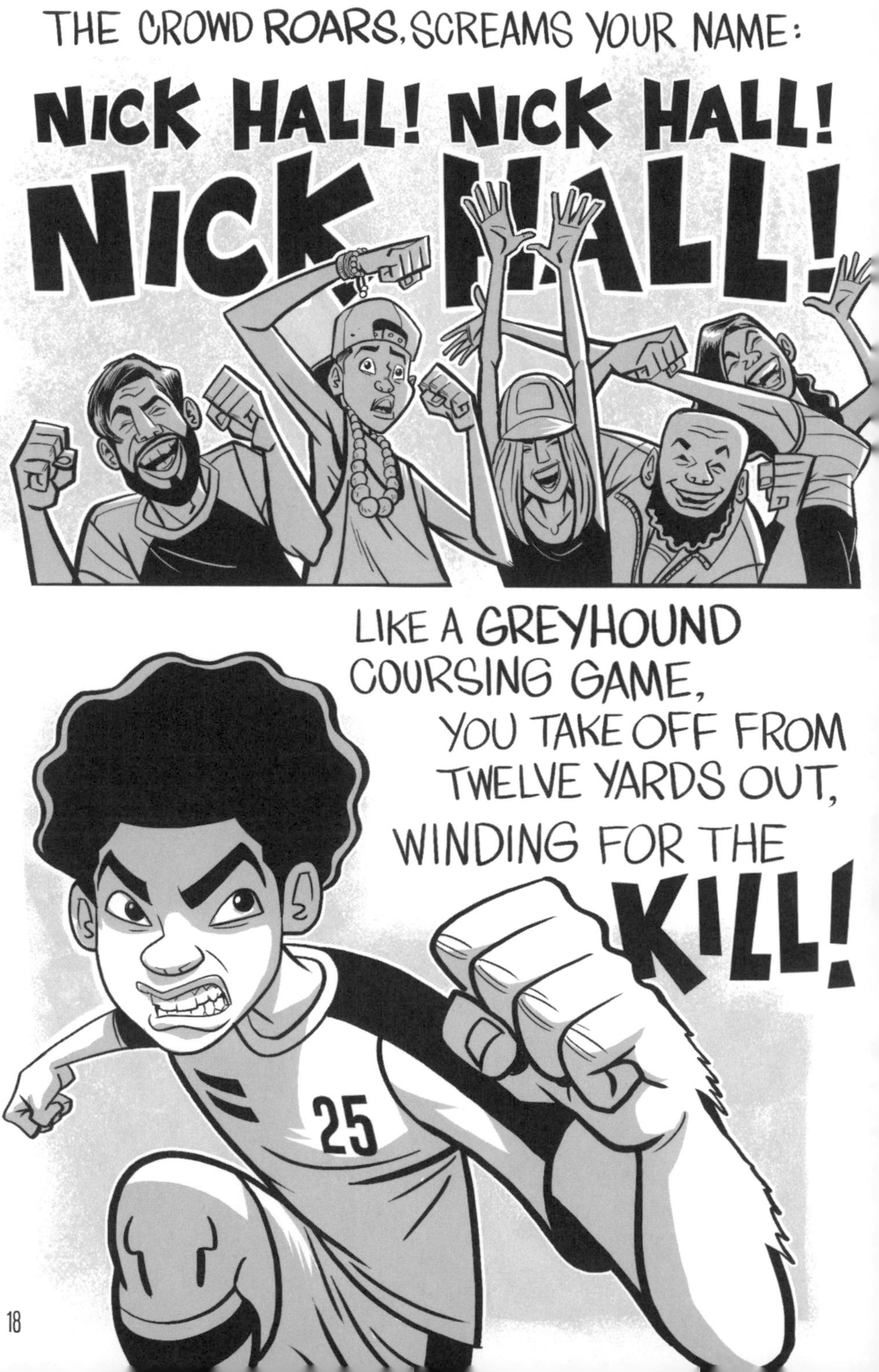
THE CROWD ROARS, SCREAMS YOUR NAME:
NICK HALL! NICK HALL!
NICK HALL!
LIKE A GREYHOUND COURSING GAME,
YOU TAKE OFF FROM TWELVE YARDS OUT,
WINDING FOR THE
KILL!
25

BUT RIGHT BEFORE THE WINNING KICK OF YOUR **BARCELONA DEBUT,**

MS. HARDWICK STREAKS ACROSS THE FIELD IN HER **HEELS** YELLING:

NICHOLAS HALL, PAY ATTENTION!

THE THING ABOUT DAYDREAMING

IN CLASS IS YOU FORGET WHAT WAS HAPPENING JUST BEFORE **NINETY THOUSAND** FANS STARTED **CHEERING** YOU TO VICTORY.

SO EVERYTHING BLURS WHEN YOUR BEST FRIEND WHISPERS FROM BEHIND,

SHE'S TALKING TO YOU, BRO, AND YOUR TEACHER **SLAMS** YOU WITH A QUESTION THAT MAKES NO SENSE:

THE EXPRESSION "TO NIP SOMETHING IN THE BUD" IS AN EXAMPLE OF WHAT, NICHOLAS?

UH, TO NIP IT IN THE BUTT IS AN EXAMPLE OF HOW TO GET **SLAPPED** BY A GIRL, YOU REPLY, AS CONFUSED AS A **CHAMELEON** IN A BAG OF **GUMMY WORMS,**

WHICH SENDS ALMOST EVERYONE IN CLASS INTO FITS OF CONTAGIOUS **SNICKERING.**

EVERYONE EXCEPT **MS. HARDWICK.**

BUSTED

NICHOLAS, I'VE WARNED YOU ABOUT NOT PAYING ATTENTION IN MY CLASS. THIS IS YOUR FINAL WARNING.

NEXT TIME, IT'S DOWN TO THE OFFICE.

NOW, CAN ANYONE ANSWER THE QUESTION CORRECTLY?

I CAN, I CAN, MS. HARDWICK, SAYS **WINNIFRED**, THE TEACHER'S PET (AND A PAIN IN THE **CLASS**).

WHAT IS THE CORRECT PHRASE, **WINNIFRED**?

NIP IT IN THE BUD, NOT BUTT, MS. HARDWICK, SHE ANSWERS, THEN ADDS, SORTA LIKE WHEN YOU PRUNE A FLOWER IN THE BUDDING STAGE, TO KEEP IT FROM GROWING.

THEN SHE ROLLS HER EYES.

IN **YOUR** DIRECTION.

PRECISELY. IT IS A **METAPHOR** FOR DEALING WITH A PROBLEM WHEN IT IS STILL SMALL AND BEFORE IT GROWS INTO SOMETHING **LARGER**, MS. HARDWICK SAYS, LOOKING DEAD AT **YOU**.

IRONICALLY, NICHOLAS, BY NOT PAYING ATTENTION, YOU HAVE **STUMBLED** UPON ANOTHER LITERARY DEVICE CALLED A **MALAPROPISM.** *

DO YOU KNOW WHAT IT MEANS?

AND OF COURSE YOU DO, BUT BEFORE YOU CAN TELL HER **WINNIFRED** RAISES HER HAND AND STARTS SPELLING IT: M-A-L-A-P-R-O-P-I-S-M, FROM THE FRENCH TERM MAL à PROPOS, MEANING WHEN A PERSON, OR IN THIS CASE, A BOY, USES A WORD THAT SOUNDS LIKE ANOTHER JUST TO BE **FUNNY**.

EXCELLENT, WINNIFRED, AND SINCE YOU'RE SUCH A COMEDIAN, NICHOLAS, MS. HARDWICK HOWLS, HOW ABOUT YOU FINISH READING THE ADVENTURES OF HUCKLEBERRY FINN AND FIND AN EXAMPLE OF A MALAPROPISM IN THE TEXT TO PRESENT IN CLASS NEXT WEEK.
HUCKLEBERRY
OF
FINN
ARRGGHH!
*MALAPROPISM [MAL-UH-PROP-IZ-UHM] NOUN: THE AMUSING AND LUDICROUS MISUSE OF A WORD, ESPECIALLY BY CONFUSION WITH ONE OF A SIMILAR SOUND. HERE'S AN EXAMPLE: MY ENGLISH TEACHER, MS. HARDWICK, IS A WOLF IN CHEAP CLOTHING.

AFTER SCHOOL

BETTER PAY ATTENTION, OR MS. HARDWICK'S GONNA GIVE YOU A GOOD KICK IN THE GRASS, COBY SAYS.

THAT WAS A **MALAPROP**, HE JOKES. **I KNOW WHAT IT WAS!**

WANNA PLAY SOCCER? HE ASKS.

OF COURSE YOU DO, BUT YOU CAN'T BECAUSE IT'S **TUESDAY** AND YOU HAVE A RIDICULOUS, **MIND-NUMBING** TWO-HOUR SPECIAL CLASS THAT YOUR MOM SIGNED YOU UP FOR THAT YOU CAN'T WAIT TO GET TO BECAUSE YOU GET TO SPEND TWO HOURS IN A ROOM WITH **APRIL.**

CAN'T TODAY, YOU LIE. GOTTA CATCH UP ON SOME **HOMEWORK.**

AT MISS QUATTLEBAUM'S SCHOOL OF BALLROOM DANCE AND ETIQUETTE

THE BOYS MUST ADDRESS THE GIRLS AS **MILADY**.

MILADY, MAY I TAKE YOUR COAT? MILADY, MAY I PLEASE HAVE THIS DANCE? MILADY, SORRY MY HANDS ARE **CLAMMY**!

AFTER YOU LEARN HOW TO PROPERLY SHAKE HANDS,

(FIRM, BUT GENTLE. NOT LIMP, LIKE A WET NOODLE. UP AND DOWN, FOR TWO TO FIVE SECONDS.)

QUATTLEBAUM CHOOSES DANCE PARTNERS. WHEN SHE GETS TO YOU, THERE ARE TWO GIRLS LEFT:

APRIL, AND A GIRL WITH CHRONIC **HALITOSIS**. GUESS WHO YOU GET?

YUCK.

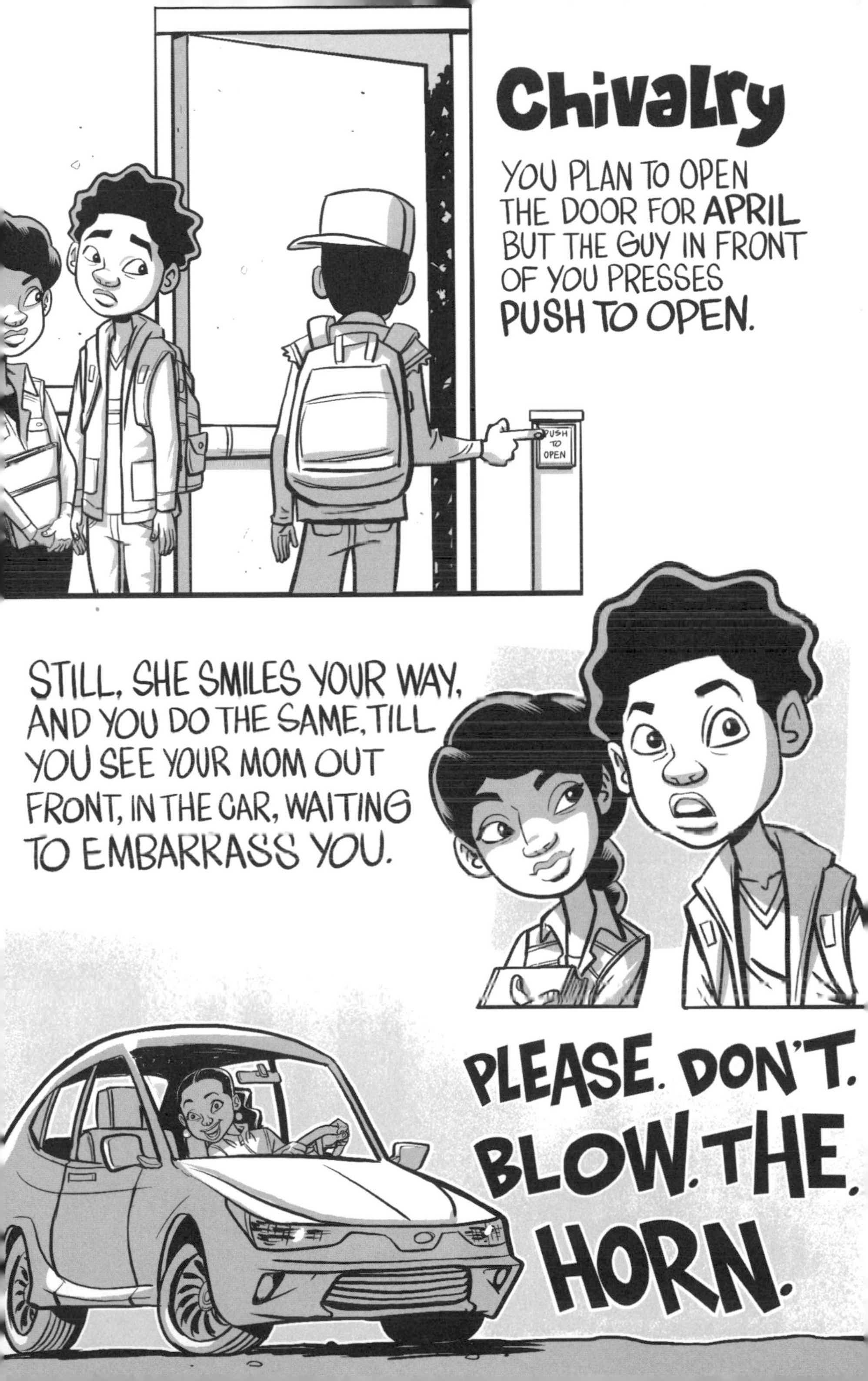
Chivalry
YOU PLAN TO OPEN THE DOOR FOR APRIL BUT THE GUY IN FRONT OF YOU PRESSES PUSH TO OPEN.
PUSH TO OPEN
STILL, SHE SMILES YOUR WAY, AND YOU DO THE SAME, TILL YOU SEE YOUR MOM OUT FRONT, IN THE CAR, WAITING TO EMBARRASS YOU.
PLEASE. DON'T. BLOW. THE. HORN.

HI, NICK.
UH, HEL...LO, UH, APRIL

THAT WAS A FUN CLASS, WASN'T IT?
...

SORRY WE DIDN'T GET TO DANCE **TONIGHT**.
UH...YEAH...I...UH.

DO YOU WANT MY NUMB—

**BEEEEEP
BEEEEEP
BWONNNK!**

HI, I'M NICK'S MOM, NICE TO MEET YOU, MOM SCREAMS OUT THE PASSENGER WINDOW AS YOU JUMP IN.

HI, MRS. HALL.
HELLO, DARLING, WHAT'S YOUR—
MOM, STOP. BYE, APRIL.
PLEASE, MOM, DRIVE.
ARGGH!

THE PACT

NINTH GRADE IS FIVE MONTHS FROM NOW WHEN YOU AND COBY HAVE **VOWED** TO HAVE A GIRLFRIEND OR DIE.

EVER SINCE FIRST GRADE

YOU AND COBY HAVE BEEN AS TIGHT AS A PAIR OF SHIN GUARDS.

STAR FOOTBALLERS AND ALWAYS FRIENDS, UNTIL NOW.

EVEN THOUGH YOU'RE ON THE SAME INDOOR SOCCER TEAM (WHICH IS COOL), FOR THE FIRST TIME EVER, YOU PLAY FOR DIFFERENT TRAVEL CLUBS (WHICH IS NOT).

29

SEE, YOU BOTH TRIED OUT FOR THE UNDER **15**.

YOU MADE THE **A** TEAM.

HE DIDN'T.

BUT THERE WAS NO **FREAKIN'** WAY THE **GREAT** COBY WAS PLAYING ON THE **B** TEAM.

SO HIS MOM DROVE HIM **THIRTY MILES** TO TRY OUT FOR ANOTHER CLUB,

AND NOW THE MOST **DANGEROUS** PLAYER ON THE **RIVAL SOCCER CLUB** ALSO HAPPENS TO BE YOUR **BEST FRIEND.**

BEST FRIEND

COBY LEE IS FROM SINGAPORE. SORTA.

HE WAS BORN THERE, LIKE HIS DAD, BUT HIS MOM'S FROM GHANA,

WHICH IS WHERE HE LEARNED *fútbol* BEFORE THEY MOVED HERE.

ALL BEFORE **COBY** TURNED FIVE.

YOU ABSOLUTELY LOVE SOCCER. BUT COBY'S MARRIED TO IT.

COMMITTED LIKE BREATHING TO IT.

IT'S ALL HE **TALKS** AND **THINKS** ABOUT.

31

IN MATH CLASS HE MADE A PIE CHART OF THE **WINNINGEST WORLD CUP JERSEY NUMBERS** OF THE PAST FIFTY YEARS.

HALF OF HIS ROOM IS PAINTED RED AND GOLD WITH COOL POSTERS OF THE **GHANA BLACK STARS.**

THE OTHER HALF, RED AND WHITE WITH POSTERS OF THE **SINGAPORE LIONS** PLASTERED ON THE WALLS. HE'S EVEN GOT A BALL AUTOGRAPHED BY **ESSIEN,** WHO HE MET ON HIS LAST TRIP TO **GHANA.**

UNFORTUNATELY, YOU RARELY SEE ANY OF THIS BECAUSE YOUR BEST FRIEND'S ROOM ALWAYS SMELLS LIKE **SKUNK PEE** AND **FUNKY FREAKIN' FEET.**

BRAGGING RIGHTS

AFTER PRACTICE YOU'RE PSYCHED TO CALL COBY AND BRAG ABOUT THE AWESOME LETTER YOUR COACH READ TO THE TEAM, WISHING YOU COULD SEE THE LOOK ON HIS FACE WHEN YOU DROP THE **NEWS.**

INSTEAD, WHAT DROPS IS **YOUR** MOUTH WHEN HE LAUGHS AND SAYS, YEAH, **WE GOT ONE TOO.**

THE LETTER

DEAR COACH,

YOUR TEAM IS INVITED TO COMPETE IN THE **DR PEPPER DALLAS CUP,** THE RENOWNED WORLD YOUTH SOCCER TOURNAMENT.

SINCE 1980, THE DALLAS CUP HAS GIVEN TALENTED UP-AND-COMING PLAYERS THE OPPORTUNITY TO COMPETE AGAINST MARQUEE TEAMS FROM ACROSS THE GLOBE.

NOTABLE ALUMNI INCLUDE **DAVID BECKHAM,** REAL MADRID'S **CHICHARITO,** AND THE FORMER NBA CHAMPION **HAKEEM OLAJUWON.**

MANY TOP COLLEGE AND PRO SCOUTS WILL BE IN ATTENDANCE, AS WELL AS MORE THAN 100,000 FANS.

CONGRATULATIONS ON THIS HONOR, AND WE LOOK FORWARD TO HOSTING YOU THIS SPRING.

DAD'S BACK IN TOWN

WHICH MEANS YOU'RE IN HIS STUDY SURROUNDED BY TEN-FOOT WALLS LINED WITH **BOOKS**.

YOU'RE THINKING OF APRIL/DALLAS/ANYTHING TO AVOID READING THE LAST FEW DREADFUL PAGES OF THIS DREADFUL BOOK.

ON A LARGE RED LEATHER COUCH DAD LOUNGES.

YOU'RE ON A BRICK-HARD CUSHION-LESS SEAT. EXERCISING. YOUR EYES. **BORED.**

YOU SNEAK YOUR PHONE OUT WHILE HE'S GLUED TO SOME BOOK BY A GUY NAMED **ROUSSEAU,**

WHO, IRONICALLY, ACCORDING TO **WIKIPEDIA,** IS QUOTED AS HAVING SAID,

I **HATE** BOOKS.

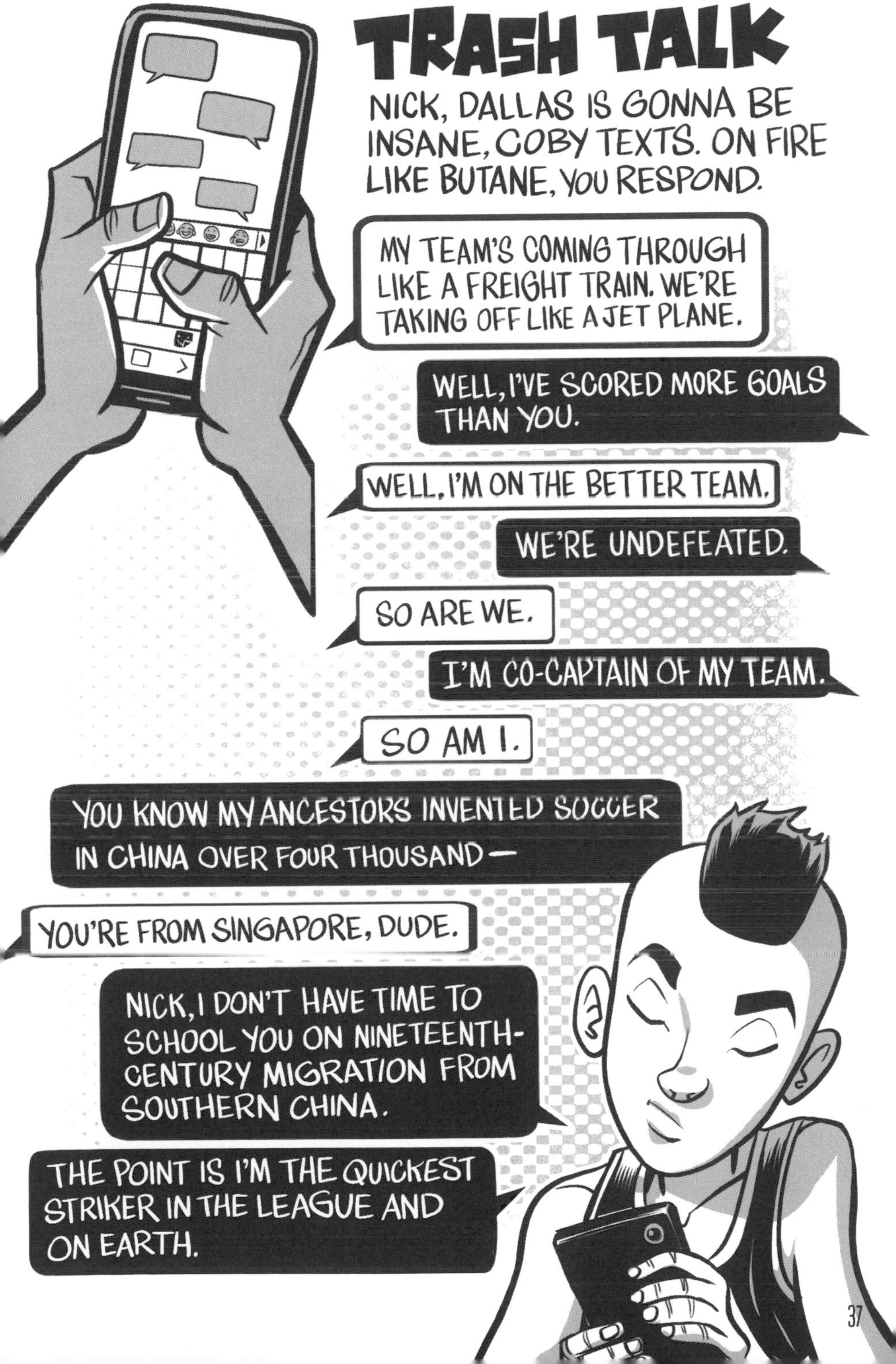
TRASH TALK
NICK, DALLAS IS GONNA BE INSANE, COBY TEXTS. ON FIRE LIKE BUTANE, YOU RESPOND.
MY TEAM'S COMING THROUGH LIKE A FREIGHT TRAIN. WE'RE TAKING OFF LIKE A JET PLANE.
WELL, I'VE SCORED MORE GOALS THAN YOU.
WELL, I'M ON THE BETTER TEAM.
WE'RE UNDEFEATED.
SO ARE WE.
I'M CO-CAPTAIN OF MY TEAM.
SO AM I.
YOU KNOW MY ANCESTORS INVENTED SOCCER IN CHINA OVER FOUR THOUSAND—
YOU'RE FROM SINGAPORE, DUDE.
NICK, I DON'T HAVE TIME TO SCHOOL YOU ON NINETEENTH-CENTURY MIGRATION FROM SOUTHERN CHINA.
THE POINT IS I'M THE QUICKEST STRIKER IN THE LEAGUE AND ON EARTH.

IN YOUR MIND!
I'M THE FASTEST BRO IN THE GAME.
COBY LIGHTNING'S MY NAME. IN FACT, I'M SO QUICK I COULD PROBABLY CATCH MYSELF.
...
NICK, YOU STILL THERE?

PUT. THE. PHONE. AWAY, NICHOLAS

AND FINISH YOUR READING.
I'M FINISHED, YOU LIE.

WHAT'D YOU THINK?
IT WAS, UH, INTERESTING.

PUT THE PHONE ON MY DESK, AND COMPLETE YOUR ASSIGNMENT.

BUT, IT'S LATE, DAD, AND I'M TIRED, AND HAVE SCHOOL TOMORROW.

DO ME A FAVOR AND STOP COMPLAINING ABOUT TRYING TO BE EXCELLENT.

WHATEVER, YOU MUMBLE.

WHAT DID YOU SAY?
NOTHING. I NEED TO USE THE BATHROOM.
THEN GO. AND BRING ME A PILLOW FROM THE GUEST ROOM.
WHY?
BECAUSE I NEED A PILLOW.
YOU'RE SLEEPING DOWN HERE?
I AM. NOW, HURRY UP.
WE STILL HAVE TO GO OVER OUR WORDS.
YOUR WORDS, YOU MUMBLE ON YOUR WAY OUT.

TROUBLE

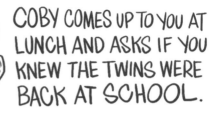

COBY COMES UP TO YOU AT LUNCH AND ASKS IF YOU KNEW THE TWINS WERE BACK AT SCHOOL.

THEN HE ASKS IF YOU KNEW ONE OF 'EM WAS IN THE LIBRARY TALKING TO **APRIL**.

 **DEAN** AND **BEN RIGGLESTON**

ARE PIT-BULL MEAN EIGHTH GRADE TYRANTS WITH **BEARDS.**
THEY USED TO PLAY **SOCCER** WITH YOU AND COBY TILL
THEY GOT KICKED OUT OF THE LEAGUE FOR LITERALLY
TACKLING OPPONENTS AND THEN,

GET THIS,

BITING THEM.

FISTS of FURY

THE TWINS LIVE DOWN THE BLOCK FROM LANGSTON HUGHES MIDDLE SCHOOL OF THE ARTS, WHICH IS WHY THEY GET TO GO HERE, SINCE THE ONLY ART THEY'RE INTERESTED IN IS **PUGILISM**,* AS EVIDENCED BY THE FLAMING-RED BOXING GLOVES THEY SOMETIMES SNEAK INTO SCHOOL TO PUNCH OTHER KIDS WITH (WHICH IS HOW THEY ENDED UP AT THE **ALTERNATIVE BEHAVIOR CENTER**, OR THE **ABC**, FOR THE PAST YEAR).

*PUGILISM [PYOO-JUH-LIZ-UHM] NOUN:
THE ART OF FIGHTING WITH YOUR FISTS; BOXING.
LIKE THE TIME THEY BOXED EACH OTHER AND DON RUPTURED DEAN'S EYEBALL, WHICH IS WHY HE WEARS A PATCH.

THE LIBRARY DOOR

SWINGS OPEN JUST AS YOU AND COBY ARRIVE.

THE TWINS **GRIT HARD.**

HEY, **PUNK,** DON SAYS. DON'T LET ME CATCH YOU WITH MY GIRL, DEAN SAYS.

WHEN YOU WALK INSIDE

THE LIBRARY, APRIL WAVES FROM THE BACK CORNER, BUT BEFORE YOU CAN WAVE BACK,

MR. MACDONALD, THE LIBRARIAN, JUMPS IN FRONT OF YOU, HOLDING A HARDCOVER BOOK IN HIS COLOSSAL LEFT HAND, A NEON GREEN BOWLING BALL IN HIS RIGHT, AND SPORTING A **WAY-TOO-BIG** 4XL TEE THAT READS:

IRONY: THE OPPOSITE OF WRINKLY

WELCOME TO THE DRAGONFLY CAFÉ

HERE FELLAS, TAKE A BOOK.

UH, NO THANKS, MR. MACDONALD. JUST CAME IN TO—

TO JOIN NERDS AND WORDS? EXCELLENT, NICK.
WE COULD USE SOME BOYS IN OUR BOOK CLUB.

MAYBE ANOTHER TIME. I DON'T REALLY DO BOOKS.

IT'S A QUICK READ—TRY IT OUT THIS WEEKEND.

CAN'T, MR. MAC, WE GOT A FUTSAL* TOURNAMENT.

A BOOK BRAWL TOURNAMENT?

FUTSAL TOURNAMENT.

YOUR FOOT'S ALL PERMANENT?

. . .

I HEARD ABOUT THAT THING IN MS. HARDWICK'S CLASS. YOU KNOW I'M THE KING OF **MALAPROPISMS.** UH, O-KAY.

WHAT'S UP WITH THE BOWLING BALL, MR. MAC?

BIG GAME THIS WEEKEND TOO. GOT TO GET MY **MATCH-PLAY MOJO** ON.

*FUTSAL [FOOT-SAUL] NOUN: INDOOR SOCCER PLAYED WITH FIVE PLAYERS ON EACH SIDE. WE HAVE OUR LAST **FUTSAL** TOURNAMENT THIS WEEK, THEN TRAVEL SOCCER CLUB REVS UP.

I DON'T EVEN KNOW WHAT THAT MEANS.
SO, COBY, YOU WANT TO JOIN THE BOOK CLUB?

PASS, COBY SAYS, LAUGHING. MAYBE IF YOU
CHANGED THE NAME TO **BOOKS** AND **BABES**
I MIGHT JOIN.

LET US SEE **WHAT'S IN YOUR DRAGONFLY** BOX AND
WE'LL JOIN, YOU SAY, BEFORE THE MAC STARTS,

GET THIS,

RAPPING:

HEY, DJ, DROP THAT BEAT

THE MAC DRINKS TEA IN A DRAGONFLY MUG.
ON THE LIBRARY FLOOR IS A DRAGONFLY RUG.

THE DOOR IS COVERED WITH DRAGONFLY
PICS, 'CAUSE SKIP TO THE MAC IS
DRAGONFLY SICK.

SOMETIMES I WEAR A
DRAGONFLY HAT.

GOT DRAGONFLY THIS
AND DRAGONFLY THAT.

AROUND MY ROOM ARE
DRAGONFLY CLOCKS.

BUT PLEASE DON'T
TOUCH MY DRAGONFLY
BOX.

'CAUSE IF YOU DO
I MIGHT GET CROSS.

RESPECT THE MAC,
DRAGONFLY **BOSS!**

SKIP MACDONALD

THE MAC IS A CORNY-JOKE-CRACKING, SEVEN-FOOT BOWLING FANATIC WITH A REDDISH MOHAWK WHO WEARS FUNNY T-SHIRTS AND HIGH-TOP CONVERSE SNEAKERS.

HE USED TO BE A RAP PRODUCER, BUT NOW HE ONLY LISTENS TO WACK ELEVATOR MUSIC, BECAUSE, HE SAYS, HIP-HOP IS DEAD.

WHEN I ASK HIM WHO KILLED IT, HE SAYS: RINGTONES AND OBJECTIFICATION.

WHICH IS REASON #1 WHY HE LEFT THE MUSIC BUSINESS AT AGE TWENTY-NINE, TO BECOME, **GET THIS,** A **LIBRARIAN?!**

REASON #2 IS THE BRAIN SURGERY HE HAD TWO YEARS AGO THAT LEFT HIM WITH A SCAR THAT RUNS ACROSS HIS HEAD FROM HIS LEFT EAR TO HIS RIGHT.

BUT HE'S THE COOLEST ADULT IN OUR SCHOOL, AND TO PROVE IT, HE'S GOT A GRAMMY AWARD FOR BEST RAP SONG SITTING RIGHT AT CHECKOUT, IN PLAIN VIEW FOR EVERYONE TO SEE AND TOUCH.

PLUS, HE'S WON TEACHER OF THE YEAR MORE TIMES THAN BRAZIL HAS WON THE WORLD CUP.

(AND HE'S NOT EVEN A TEACHER.) SO WHEN HE GETS ALL GEEKED ABOUT HIS NERDY BOOK CLUB OR BREAKS INTO SOME RANDOM RAP IN THE MIDDLE OF A CONVERSATION, MOST PEOPLE SMILE OR CLAP, BECAUSE WE'RE ALL JUST HAPPY THE MAC'S STILL ALIVE.

HUCKLEBERRY FINN-ISHED

GREAT DISCUSSION TODAY, CLASS. I'M SURE YOU ALL SEE WHY **MARK TWAIN** IS ONE OF OUR GREATEST LITERARY TREASURES, MS. HARDWICK SAYS.

WITH ONLY FIVE MINUTES LEFT IN CLASS, IT'S PROBABLE SHE'S FORGOTTEN THE ASSIGNMENT SHE GAVE YOU, WHICH MEANS YOU'RE OFF THE **HOOK**.

TOMORROW, WE WILL BEGIN ANOTHER CLASSIC OF CHILDREN'S LITERATURE. ONE OF MY FAVORITES, **TUCK EVERLASTING.**

AND YOUR LAUGHTER GUSHES LIKE AN OPEN FIRE HYDRANT 'CAUSE YOU COULD HAVE SWORN YOU HEARD AN **F,**

INSTEAD OF **T.**

I SEE OUR COMEDIAN IS BACK. WOULD YOU LIKE TO SHARE WHAT'S SO FUNNY WITH THE REST OF THE CLASS?
UH, NO THANKS, I'M GOOD.
WINEY, THE KNOW-IT-ALL, A.K.A. WINNIFRED, THE GIRL WHO BEAT YOU IN THE ELEMENTARY SCHOOL SPELLING BEE, RAISES HER HAND:
MS. HARDWICK, WASN'T NICK SUPPOSED TO PRESENT A MALAPROPISM TO US TODAY? SHE WHINES.
ARGGH!

THANK YOU, WINNIFRED, MS. HARDWICK INTERRUPTS.

NICK, HERE'S YOUR CHANCE TO BE **FUNNY**.

WERE YOU ABLE TO FIND A **MALAPROPISM** IN **HUCKLEBERRY FINN?**

NO, YOU SAY, HANDING HER THE ASSIGNMENT.

I ACTUALLY FOUND **TWO**.

[redacted]

READS

[redacted]

JEST

[redacted]

LIKE

[redacted]

A

[redacted]

FUNERAL ORGIE

[redacted]

I

[redacted]

SHOVED

[redacted]

IT

[redacted]

DOWN

[redacted]

THE

[redacted]

T [redacted] O [redacted] I [redacted] L [redacted] ET

[redacted]

CLASS ENDS

WHEN MS. HARDWICK READS YOUR ASSIGNMENT THEN RUNS INTO THE HALLWAY CACHINNATING* LIKE SHE'S ABOUT TO PEE IN HER POLYESTER.

* **CACHINNATE** [KAK-UH-NAYT] VERB: TO LAUGH LOUDLY. IN **HUCK FINN**, MARK TWAIN MISUSED THE WORDS "ORGIES" FOR "OBSEQUIES" (WHICH MEANS "CEREMONIES"), AND "JEST" FOR "JUST" (WHICH MEANS, UH, "JUST"). GET IT? YEAH, ME EITHER, BUT HARDWICK APPARENTLY DID, 'CAUSE WE CAN STILL HEAR HER CACHINNATING, SO I GUESS MY JOB'S DONE. NICK HALL, SCORE!

USUALLY AT DINNER

MOM'S ASKING RANDOM QUESTIONS ABOUT GIRLS AND SCHOOL, DAD'S TALKING ABOUT SOME NEW, WEIRD WORD HE'S FOUND, AND YOU'RE EATING AS FAST AS YOU CAN, SO YOU CAN FINISH AND GET ONLINE TO PLAY **FIFA** WITH COBY.

BUT TONIGHT IS DIFFERENT.

THE FOOD'S GOOD, AS USUAL—FETTUCCINE ALFREDO WITH **JUMBO SHRIMP**, CORN ON THE **COB**, GARLIC BREAD STICKS— BUT, **GET THIS,** NO ONE'S SAYING A **WORD.**

IT'S LIKE CHURCH DURING **PRAYER.**

DEAD SILENCE. **CRICKETS.**

SOMETHING'S NOT **RIGHT.**

BREAKING THE SILENCE

CAN I HAVE TWO HUNDRED DOLLARS TO TAKE TO THE DALLAS CUP? YOU ASK.

THAT'S ABSURD, NICKY, MOM ANSWERS.

COBY'S DAD IS GIVING HIM **FIVE HUNDRED.**

IT'S NOT FOR A WHILE. WE'LL DISCUSS THIS LATER, SHE ADDS. DAD DOESN'T SAY ANYTHING, WHICH CONFIRMS THAT SOMETHING'S UP, 'CAUSE HE **ALWAYS. HAS. SOMETHING. TO SAY.**

THEN IT'S ALL **HUSH-HUSH** AGAIN.

YOU CLEAR THE TABLE, MOM HUGS YOU LONGER THAN USUAL,

THEN YOU HEAD UPSTAIRS TO CRAM FOR YOUR MATH TEST WHEN YOU HEAR DAD, FROM THE LIVING ROOM, SAY,

NICHOLAS, CAN YOU COME IN HERE FOR A MINUTE?

YOUR MOTHER AND I NEED TO TALK WITH YOU,

AND YOU PRAY THEY DIDN'T FIND OUT ABOUT THE LAMP YOU BROKE WHILE KICKING THE BALL IN YOUR ROOM.

NO HEADS-UP

WHEN MOM SAYS SHE'S DECIDED TO GO BACK TO WORK, YOU'RE NOT TOO SURPRISED, 'CAUSE YOU KNOW HOW MUCH SHE MISSES BEING AROUND HORSES SINCE DAD MOVED THE FAMILY TO THE CITY FOR HIS TEACHING JOB.

WHEN SHE SAYS SHE'S DECIDED TO TAKE A JOB IN KENTUCKY, IT JOLTS YOU, 'CAUSE MOVING AWAY FROM YOUR FRIENDS AND TEAMMATES IN THE MIDDLE OF THE SCHOOL YEAR IS **VICIOUS**.

BUT WHEN SHE SAYS,

NICKY, YOUR FATHER AND I ARE **SEPARATING,**

IT'S LIKE A BOMBSHELL DROPS RIGHT IN THE CENTER OF YOUR HEART AND SPLATTERS ALL ACROSS YOUR LIFE.

THOUGHT
IT DOES NOT TAKE A MATH GENIUS TO UNDERSTAND THAT WHEN YOU SUBTRACT A MOTHER FROM THE EQUATION WHAT REMAINS IS NEGATIVE.

BROKEN

AFTER YOU FINISH CRYING AND THE SADNESS FINDS
A HOME IN WHAT'S LEFT OF YOUR HEART,
YOU ASK HER WHEN SHE'S LEAVING YOU.

I'M NOT LEAVING **YOU**, NICKY. I HAVE TO GO OUT NEXT
WEEK, MEET WITH THE RACING TEAM, BUT I'LL BE BACK
EVERY OTHER WEEKEND UNTIL THE TRIPLE CROWN,
AND THEN I'M HOME FOR THE SUMMER AND WE'LL
FIGURE OUT HOW TO FIX ALL THIS.

HOW IS SHE GONNA FIX THIS SHATTERED HEART,
YOU WONDER?

FOR THE REST OF THE WEEK

YOU CAN'T SLEEP, YOUR HEAD ACHES, YOUR STOMACH'S A WRECK, YOUR SOUL'S ON FIRE, YOUR PARENTS ARE CLUELESS, YOU FALL ASLEEP IN CLASS, YOU FAIL THE MATH TEST, YOU'RE SCARED TO TALK TO **APRIL**, AND YOU'RE TRAPPED IN A CAGE OF MISERY WITH FREEDOM NOWHERE IN SIGHT.

IF NOT FOR SOCCER, WHAT'D BE THE POINT?

CONVERSATION BEFORE THE MATCH

YOU OKAY, BRO?
YEAH, I'M FINE.

IT'S OKAY TO CRY IF YOU WANT. I HEARD IT KILLS BACTERIA.
NOBODY'S CRYING.

DUDE, PARENTS SUCK.
YEP.

THEY TELL YOU WHY?
SOMETHING ABOUT HOW THEY STILL LOVE EACH OTHER BUT THEY DON'T LIKE EACH OTHER.

THAT SOUNDS LIKE MY PARENTS, EXCEPT THEY DON'T LOVE EACH OTHER EITHER.
YEAH, WELL, THEY'RE SCREWING UP MY LIFE.

SO, WHO ARE YOU GONNA LIVE WITH?
SHE'S MOVING TO KENTUCKY.

WHAT'S IN **KENTUCKY?**
THE HORSE.

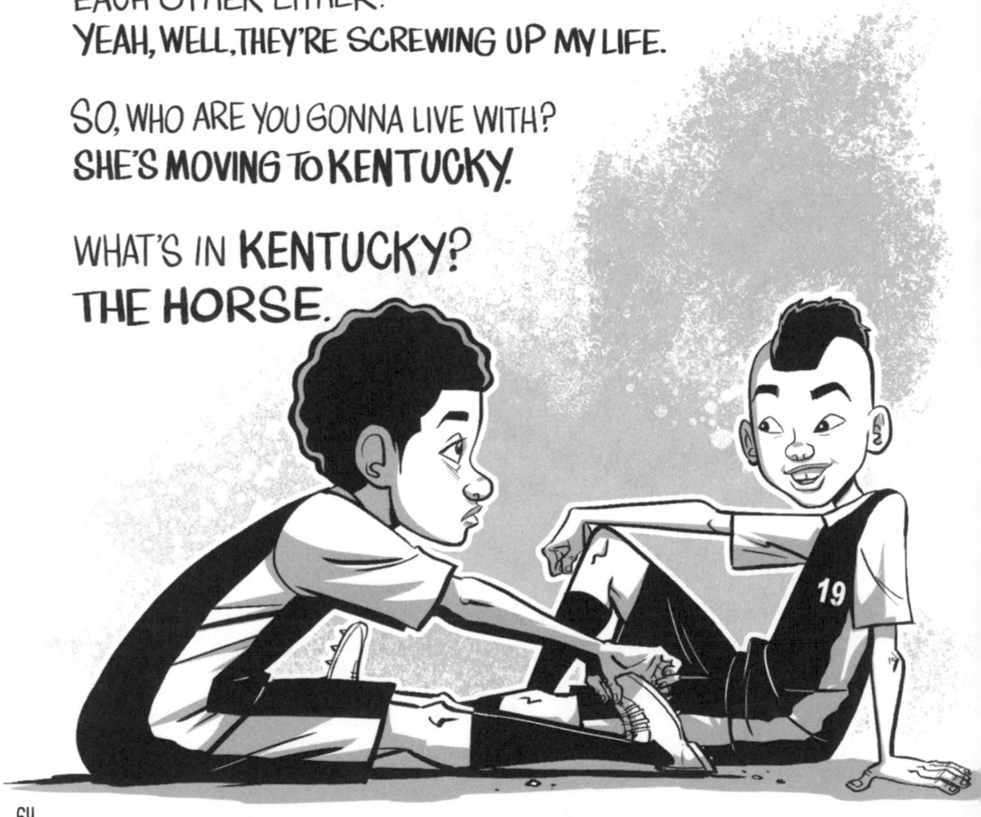
19

SO, WHAT ARE YOU GONNA DO?
SHE SAYS I'LL BE BETTER, FOR NOW, LIVING WITH MY DAD.

SHE'S PROBABLY RIGHT. DO THEY EVEN HAVE SOCCER IN KENTUCKY?
DUDE, ME AND HIM ALONE IS A NIGHTMARE.

BUT YOU CAN'T LEAVE IN THE MIDDLE OF SOCCER SEASON.
IT'S NOT LIKE SHE EVEN ASKED ME TO COME WITH HER.

WAIT, IF YOUR MOM'S MOVING, WHO'S GONNA TAKE US TO SCHOOL.
I DON'T WANNA TALK ABOUT IT.

BRO, DON'T TELL ME WE GOTTA TAKE THE CITY BUS.
WHY CAN'T YOUR DAD TAKE US?
WHY CAN'T YOUR MOM?

YOU KNOW SHE WORKS EARLY MORNINGS. PLUS HER CAR IS ORANGE,
I'M NOT GOING OUT LIKE THAT.
THEN WE BETTER GET BUS PASSES.

SORRY YOUR PARENTS ARE SPLITTING UP,
BRO, BUT THIS REALLY SUCKS.
I'M NOT TRIPPIN'. THERE'S COACH, LET'S GO.

65

PLAYING SOCCER

IS LIKE NEVER HITTING PAUSE ON YOUR FAVORITE NINETY-MINUTE MOVIE BUT **FUTSAL** IS LIKE FAST-FORWARD FOR FORTY SUPERCHARGED **MINUTES.**

GAME ONE ZIPS BY LIKE A **PRONGHORN ANTELOPE,** FAST AND **FURIOUS,** AND JUST WHEN WE WIND THE CORNER TO A RECORD THIRTEEN-GOAL SHUTOUT

OUR GOALIE GOES DOWN WITH A, GET THIS, **BROKEN PINKIE TOE.**

GAME TWO

HOME **11:29** GUEST
4 PERIOD **4**
2

THEIR BEST PLAYER ATTACKS,
STEALS THE BALL,
PASSES IT DOWN COURT
TO AN OPEN MAN,
WHO SHOOTS IT

JUST LEFT OF OUR GOALIE,
WHO NORMALLY PLAYS
MIDFIELDER:

BUZZER.
BEATER.

NO PROBLEMO

COACH SAYS WE MUST WIN OUR FINAL GAME TO ADVANCE TO THE NEXT ROUND OF THE **TOURNAMENT**.

WE SAY, NO PROBLEM.

WHEN OUR OPPONENTS RUN OUT ON THE HARDWOOD WITH THEIR PONYTAILS AND MATCHING PINK SHIRTS AND SOCKS, CARRYING GYM BAGS (PROBABLY FILLED WITH GLITTERED **SMARTPHONES**),

WE SAY, NO PROBLEM.

PROBLEMO

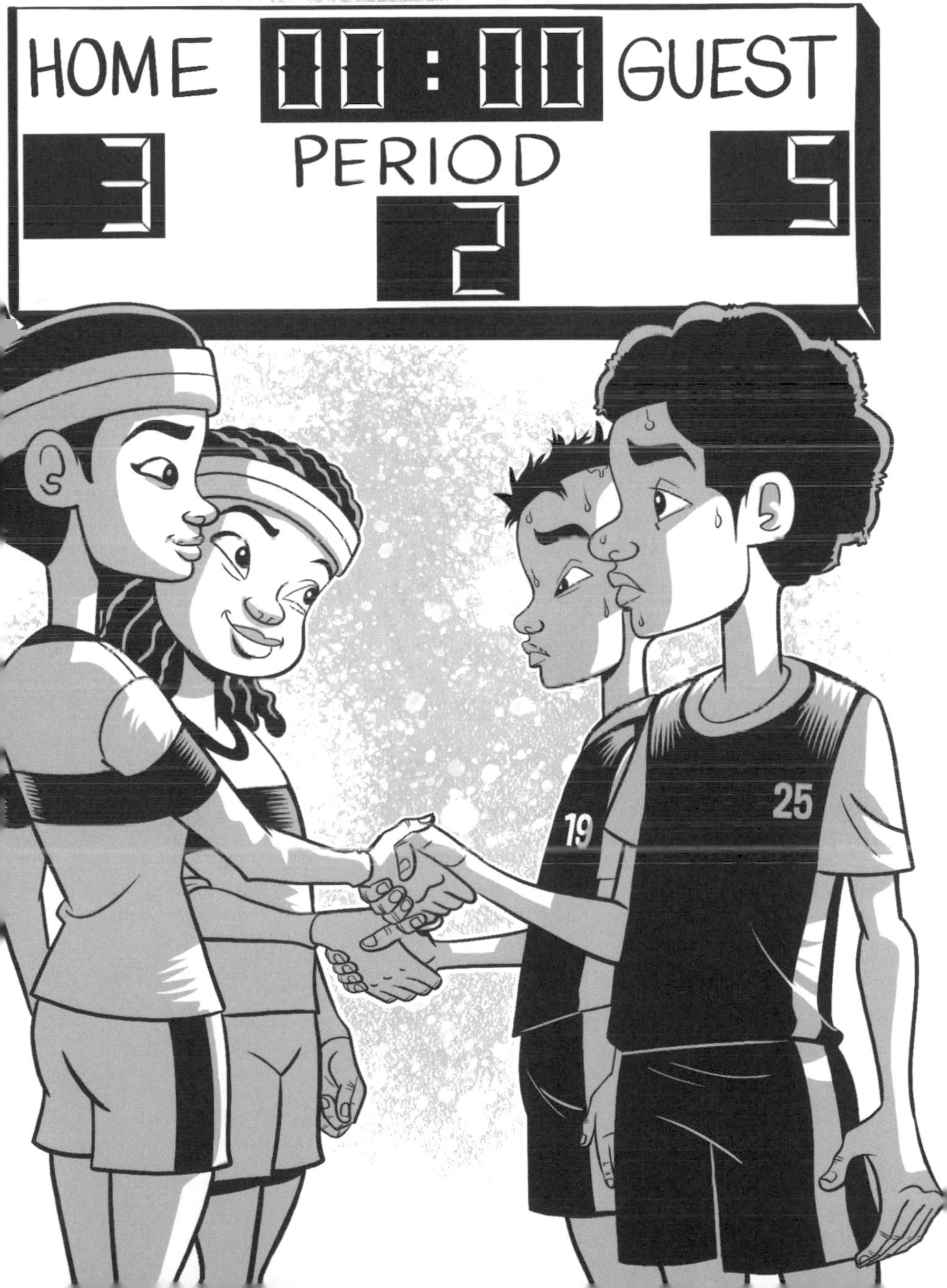
HOME
00 : 00
GUEST
3
PERIOD
2
5
19
25

CONVERSATION WITH MOM

HOW'S YOUR DINNER? **IT'S OKAY.**

IT'S YOUR FAVORITE. **THANKS.**

I HEARD FROM **MS. HARDWICK.** SHE SAID YOU FELL ASLEEP IN CLASS. **TWICE.**

...

I KNOW THIS IS TOUGH, NICKY, BUT YOU CAN'T SLACK OFF. **I WASN'T ASLEEP. I WAS DAYDREAMING.**

MAYBE SOCCER IS TAKING TOO MUCH OF YOUR TIME. **IT'S NOT.**

... ...

I SAW SOME OF YOUR TEAMMATES CRYING AFTER THE GAME. THEY WEREN'T EVEN REALLY CRYING. IT WAS JUST **MEWLING.***

* MEWLING [MYOOL-EENG] VERB: TO CRY WEAKLY; WHIMPER. I WASN'T.

WELL, THEY SHOULDA BEEN **BAWLING**, 'CAUSE THOSE GIRLS BEAT Y'ALL LIKE RENTED **MULES**.

...

THEY WHOOPED Y'ALL BAD, SHE SAYS, LAUGHING AND TICKLING.

STOP, MOM, IT'S NOT FUNNY.

YOU'RE RIGHT, THAT BEATDOWN WAS NOT FUNNY AT ALL.

THEY'RE RANKED NUMBER ONE IN THE STATE.

NOBODY TOLD US THAT.

NOBODY SHOULD HAVE TO TELL YOU TO PLAY HARD.

YOUR TEAM JUST GAVE UP, NICKY.

YOU MEAN LIKE YOU AND DAD...JUST GAVE UP?

DEAR NICK

I'M SENDING OUT A SEARCH TEAM TO LOOK FOR YOUR SMILE, 'CAUSE IT'S BEEN MISSING. HUGS, APRIL F.

YOU WANT TO TALK ABOUT APRIL, BUT COBY'S MIND IS ON THE DALLAS CUP.

THINK SHE LIKES ME?

MAYBE WE'LL GET TO MEET THE COWBOYS.

YOU THINK SHE LIKES **DEAN?**

WHAT'S YOUR HOTEL?

SHE SAID SHE LIKES MY **SMILE.**

MY COUSIN PLAYED IN THE **DALLAS CUP.**

YOUR COUSIN ELVIS, WHO DRIVES AN ICE CREAM TRUCK?
HE PLAYED MAJOR LEAGUE SOCCER FOR A YEAR, THOUGH.

WHAT SHOULD I DO ABOUT **APRIL**?
FOR STARTERS, TALK TO HER, DUDE. YOU'VE NEVER EVEN
SAID HELLO.

I HAVE **SAID HELLO. TWICE.**
ENOUGH **YAPPING**, IT'S GETTING DARK. LET'S GO PLAY SOCCER.

CAN'T. GOTTA GET HOME.
WHY?

MY MOM'S LEAVING
AFTER DINNER.
THE LAST SUPPER.

MM-HMM. LATER.
GOOD LUCK.

NOTHING GOOD ABOUT BYE

I'M SORRY, HONEY.
I DON'T UNDERSTAND. EVERYTHING WAS GOING GREAT.
Y'ALL DIDN'T GIVE ME ANY **HEADS UP.**

THIS DOESN'T CHANGE HOW MUCH WE STILL LOVE YOU.
MM-HMM.

HOW ABOUT A GAME OF **PING-PONG?**
NAH.

LOOK, NICKY, THIS IS TOUGH, I KNOW, BUT WE'LL GET
THROUGH THIS.
HOW?

I'LL BE BACK IN TWO WEEKS,
AND YOUR FATHER AND I WILL
FIGURE SOME THINGS
OUT, OKAY?

SURE.

NO CEREAL FOR DINNER, AND NO SKIPPING ETIQUETTE.
SURE.

THERE ARE BUS PASSES IN THE KITCHEN DRAWER.
MM-HMM.

ONE-WORD ANSWERS NOW, THAT'S ALL YOUR MOTHER GETS?
ARE WE DONE YET?
I HAVE SOME HOMEWORK TO FINISH.

I'M GONNA MISS YOU, HONEY.
WHAT ABOUT DAD? AREN'T YOU GONNA SAY GOODBYE TO HIM?

WE ALREADY SAID OUR GOODBYES, NICKY. NOW COME GIVE ME A **BIG HUG.**

. . .

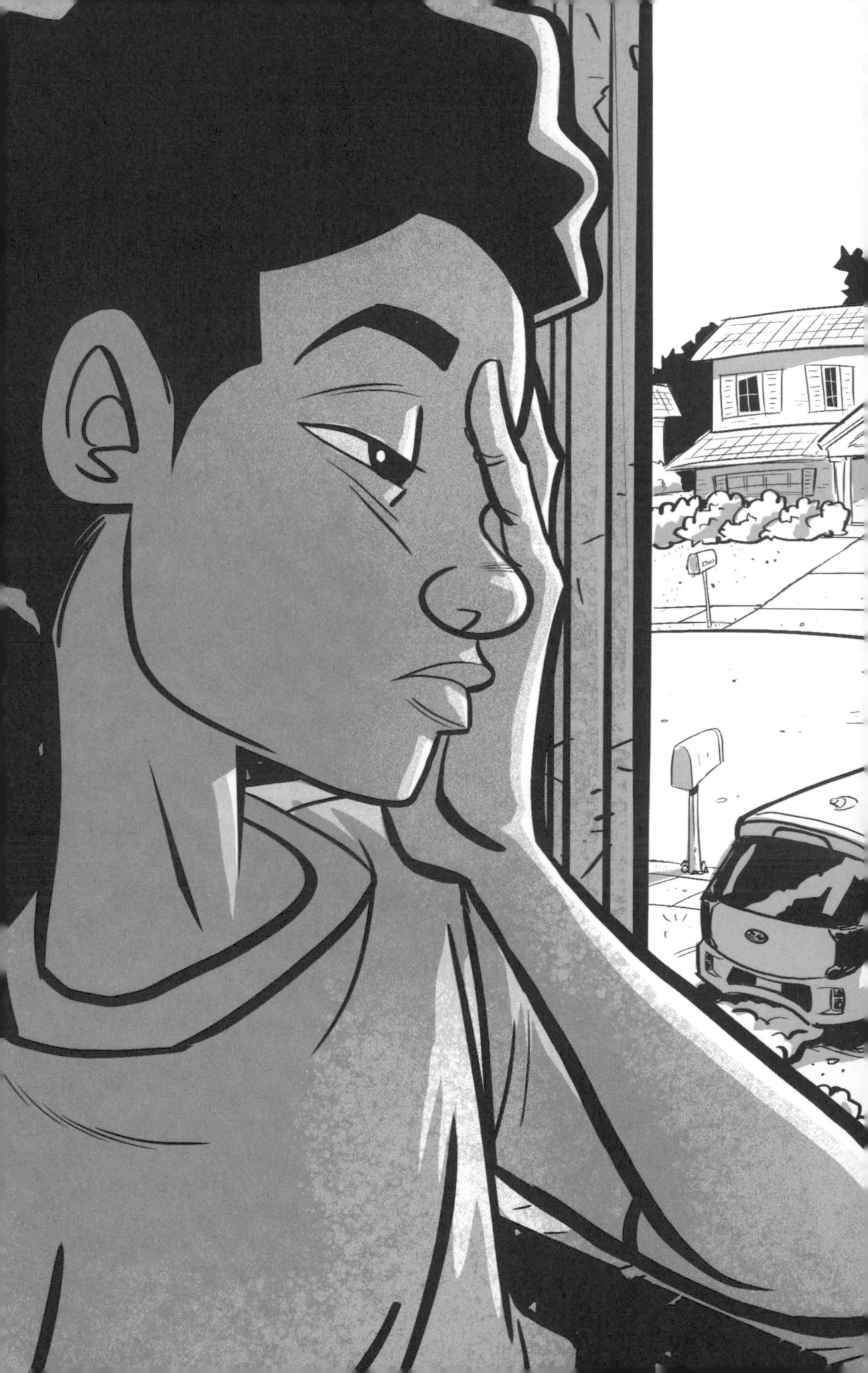

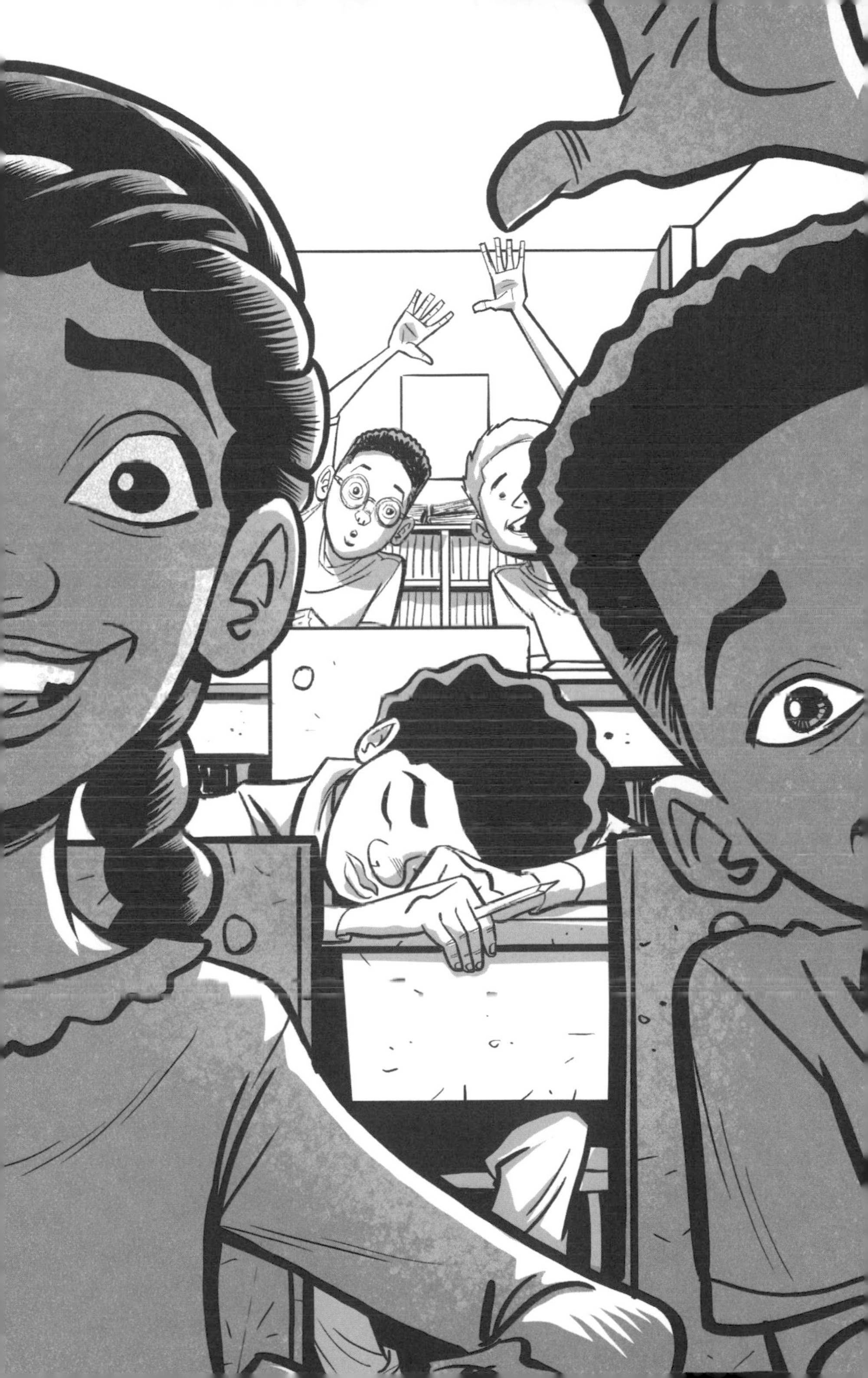

IN THE HALLWAY

AFTER CLASS YOU SEE THE MAC GRINNING LIKE HE'S JUST WON THE LOTTERY.

CHECK IT OUT, HE SAYS, HANDING YOU A SHEET OF PAPER WITH, **GET THIS,** MOST OF THE WORDS BLACKED OUT.

[redacted] A [redacted]
NEW [redacted]
READER [redacted]
KNOWS [redacted]
HOPE [redacted]
AND [redacted] HAPPINESS [redacted]
! [redacted]
THEY BECOME HUNGRY [redacted]
PUSHED
INTO THE HANDS OF [redacted] ! WE [redacted]
PROMISE [redacted]
READ [redacted]
TO [redacted]
BE [redacted]
SATISFIED [redacted]
KNOWING [redacted]

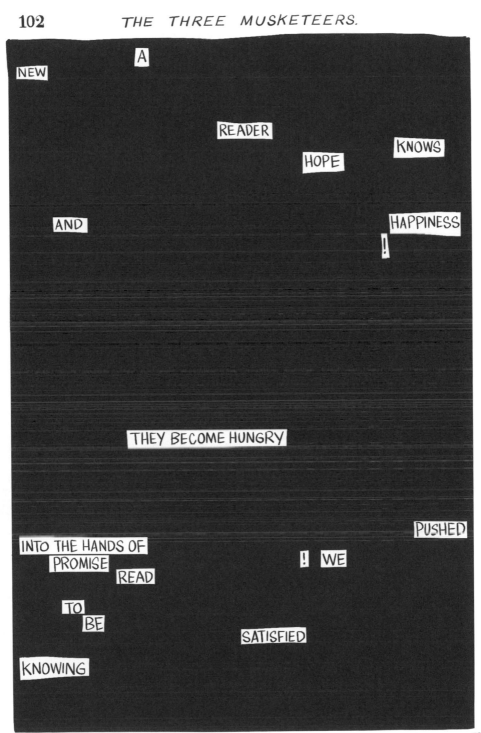

CONVERSATION WITH THE MAC

YOU INSPIRED ME, HE SAYS. PRETTY COOL, HUH?
UH, I GUESS.

MS. HARDWICK SHOWED ME
YOUR ASSIGNMENT. MAGNIFICENT!

IT WASN'T ALL THAT. I JUST DIDN'T
FEEL LIKE WRITING THREE PARAGRAPHS
ON WHY THE BOOK IS **RAGABASH**.*

DIDN'T LIKE IT, HUH?
YOU'RE MISSING OUT.
HUCKLEBERRY FINN IS A
MASTERPIECE, MY FRIEND.

MORE LIKE A DISASTER PIECE.
IT WAS WAY TOO SLOW.

HMM, YOU WANT A FASTER PIECE?
I'VE GOT SOMETHING —
UH, I'M GOOD, MR. MAC.

I'M GOING TO HOOK YOU UP, NICK.
HOW ABOUT YOU HOOK ME UP WITH
THAT **DRAGONFLY BOX**?

YOU'RE STILL SWEATING THIS LITTLE
OLD BOX? HE ASKS, HOLDING IT IN
HIS HAND.
WHY WON'T YOU TELL US WHAT'S
INSIDE, MR. MAC?

*RAGABASH [RAG-A-BASH] NOUN: WORTHLESS, RUBBISH. THE BOOK
HAS A LOT OF BAD GRAMMAR, AND MY DAD SAYS
IT GOT BANNED WHEN HE WAS IN SCHOOL BECAUSE
IT WAS RACIST. SO YEAH, RAGABASH.

MYSTERY IS GOOD FOR THE SOUL.

I WON'T TELL ANYBODY.

MAYBE, HE SAYS, THEN NUDGES YOU OUT THE LIBRARY, BEFORE YOU REALIZE HE'S PUT A BOOK IN YOUR HANDS.

ARGGH!

FIRST DINNER WITHOUT MOM

MUSTARD MAC-AND-CHEESE SMELLS AS BAD AS IT
SOUNDS, AND TASTES EVEN WORSE.

HOW WAS SCHOOL?
FINE.

DID YOU FINISH THE Rs?

...

HE KNOWS YOUR PAUSE MEANS NO.

THE GOOD COLLEGES LOOK FOR EXTRAORDINARY,
NICHOLAS. YOU NEED TO KNOW THESE WORDS IF YOU
WANT TO ATTEND A GOOD COLLEGE, NICHOLAS.
COLLEGE IS NOT FOR, LIKE, FIVE YEARS, DAD.

PLACEMENT TESTS.
APPLICATION ESSAYS.
IT'S ALL WORDS, SON.
KNOW THE WORDS AND
YOU'LL EXCEL.

NONE OF MY FRIENDS HAVE TO MEMORIZE A THOUSAND WORDS. I'M NOT LIKE YOU, DAD. MAYBE I DON'T WANT TO BE EXTRAORDINARY. MAYBE I JUST WANT TO BE ORDINARY.

THAT'S A LOAD OF CODSWALLOP.* I GIVE YOU THE DICTIONARY SO YOU'LL KNOW THE WORLD BETTER, SON. SO YOU'LL BE BETTER.

...
...

YOUR MOTHER TEXTED TODAY.
...
SHE **MISSES** YOU. DO YOU MISS HER?

SHE'S WORRIED ABOUT YOU, NICHOLAS. GIVE HER A CALL. YOU DIDN'T ANSWER MY QUESTION.

IT'S COMPLICATED. BUT WE'RE BOTH STILL HERE FOR YOU. YOU'RE NOT BOTH HERE. THAT'S THE PROBLEM.

LET'S JUST FINISH EATING. I'M DONE.

*CODSWALLOP [COD-SWAH-LUP] NOUN: SOMETHING UTTERLY SENSELESS: NONSENSE.

83

HE TELLS YOU TO TAKE THE LEFTOVERS
FOR LUNCH.

YEAH, RIGHT.

AFTER YOU TRASH THEM,

YOU CLEAR THE TABLE AND
MAKE A BACON, HAM. AND
CHEESE SANDWICH FOR
YOUR **ACTUAL** LUNCH, THEN
HEAD OFF TO NOT SLEEP
FOR THE THIRD NIGHT
IN A ROW.

MAYO

I'M SORRY

COBY SAYS.

FOR WHAT? YOU ASK.

FOR WHEN WE
BEAT Y'ALL IN
TWO WEEKS.

NOT GONNA HAPPEN, DUDE.
YOU KICK THE BALL BACK TO HIM.

I'M STARVING.
IS YOUR MOM COOKING?

NAH, BUT WE GOT
LEFTOVERS.

WATCH THIS, NICK, HE SAYS,

THEN DRIBBLE TO THE CENTER OF HIS BACKYARD AND

FLAME THROWS A BANANA KICK SO SWIFT,

IT BASICALLY SPLITS THE AIR, THEN SIZZLES RIGHT INTO HIS DOGHOUSE.

CONVERSATION

WHATCHU DOING?
**JUST CHECKING TO SEE IF THE
WARDEN CALLED.**

BRO, YOU DO KNOW YOUR
DAD'S FAMOUS.
MY DAD BLOWS.

I GOOGLED HIM. DID YOU KNOW
HE'S GOT NINE THOUSAND FOLLOWERS?
**YOU'RE GOOGLING MY DAD.
THAT'S WEIRD.**

I'M JUST SAYING, HE'S COOL. REMEMBER
THAT TIME HE TOOK US TO **FUN PARK?**
COBY, WE WERE, LIKE, SEVEN.

BUT WE HAD FUN, THOUGH. THAT FLYING
CIRCUS RIDE WAS **INSANE!**
**AT LEAST YOUR DAD DOESN'T
MAKE YOU READ THE DICTIONARY.**

IT'S HARD FOR HIM TO MAKE ME DO
ANYTHING, WHEN I ONLY SEE HIM
ONCE A YEAR.

YOUR MOM CAN COOK, THOUGH.
I LOVE HER FOOD.

MY MOM BLOWS.

LET'S CALL APRIL, HE SAYS

BUT WHEN SHE ANSWERS YOU CAN'T THINK OF ANYTHING TO SAY, SO YOU PRESS END CALL.

MAN UP, NICK.

TELL HER THAT HER SMILE SPARKLES LIKE A MIDNIGHT STAR, OR SOMETHING.

OR GIVE HER **THESE**.

THEN HE REACHES IN HIS TOP DRAWER DRAWER AND HANDS YOU, GET THIS, MILK CHOCOLATE WRAPPED IN SHINY RED AND GOLD. WHAT AM I SUPPOSED TO DO WITH TWO BARS OF CHOCOLATE, COBY?

NOT JUST ANY OLD CHOCOLATE, BRO.

ONE HUNDRED PERCENT PREMIUM DELUXE COCOA **MADE IN GHANA!**

SO SWEET IT'LL GIVE YOU A **CAVITY** JUST THINKING ABOUT IT.

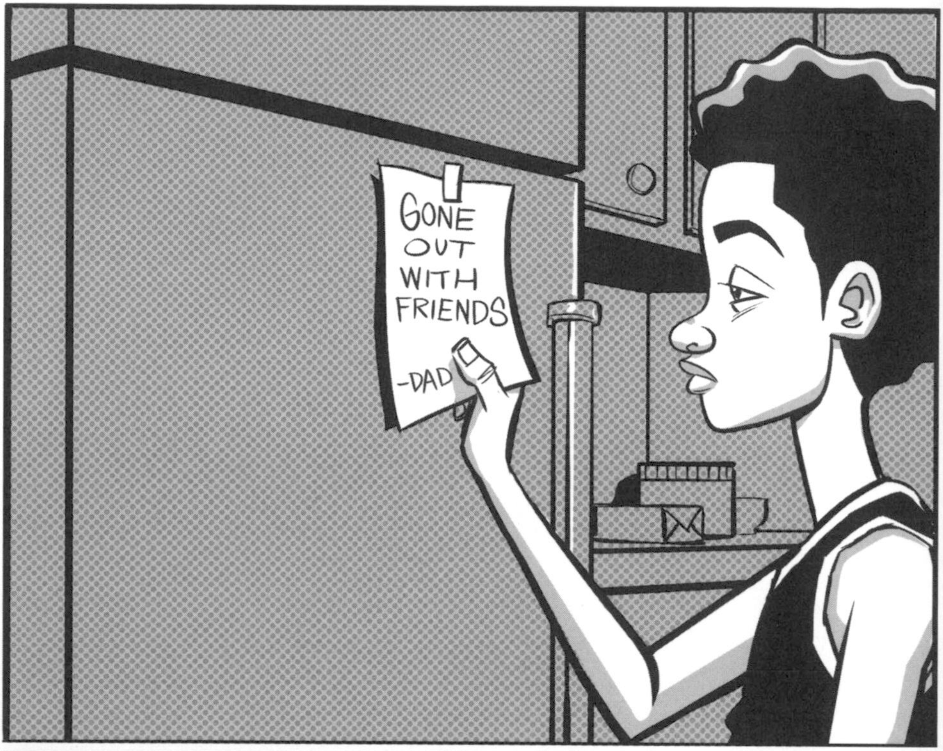
GONE OUT WITH FRIENDS
-DAD

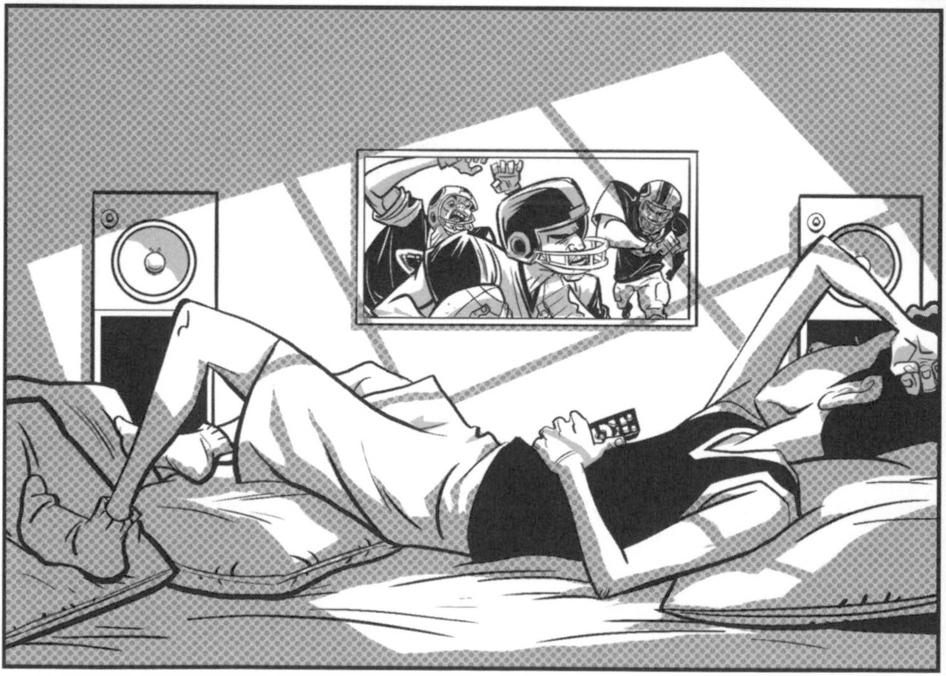

THE HOMEWORK QUESTIONS

WHERE ARE YOU GOING? HE ASKS, SITTING ON THE FRONT STOOP.

OH, HEY, DAD, YOU SAY, STARTLED. UH, LOOKS LIKE THE **STORM** **MISSED US AGAIN.** GONNA BE A SWELL WEEKEND, YOU SAY, SALUTING THE SUN, WISHING YOU HAD SNUCK OUT EARLIER AND AVOIDED THE BLAH BLAH **BLAH**.

SO YOU'RE THE **WEATHERMAN** NOW, HUH? HE ASKS, LACING HIS **RUNNING SHOES.**

YOU GOING RUNNING, DAD?

DON'T TRY TO CHANGE THE SUBJECT. DO YOU HAVE A MATCH TODAY?
THIS AFTERNOON.

SO, WHERE ARE YOU GOING?

TO MEET COBY AT THE PARK.

DID YOU **FINISH** YOUR HOMEWORK? THE **R**S?

. . .

AVERAGE PERSON KNOWS ABOUT TWELVE THOUSAND WORDS. AVERAGE PRESIDENT KNOWS TWICE THAT, HE SAYS, SOUNDING LIKE **MORGAN FREEMAN**.

EVEN GEORGE **BUSH**? YOU SAY WITH A SMIRK.

YOU WANT TO GO TO **DALLAS**, RIGHT?

I AM GOING TO DALLAS. Y'ALL ALREADY SAID I COULD GO.

YOU DO WHAT YOU **NEED** TO DO, IN ORDER TO DO WHAT YOU **WANT** TO DO. AND I SUSPECT THAT YOU STILL **NEED** TO DO SOME READING.

BUT, DAD, I SHOULDN'T HAVE TO READ ON THE **WEEKEND**. I HAVE A GAME THIS AFTERNOON, A GAME TOMORROW, PLUS THERE'S THREE MATCHES COBY AND I ARE WATCHING LATER ON TV, AND I —

READ FOR AN HOUR, THEN YOU CAN GO, HE SHOUTS, ALREADY A HALF BLOCK INTO HIS MORNING STRIDE. AND DON'T FORGET TO CALL YOUR **MOTHER**.

ARGGH!

TEXT FROM MOM

MY DEAR NICKY, I'M ASSUMING YOU'VE BEEN EATEN BY A BLACK MAMBA OR PUMMELED TO SHREDS BY A STAMPEDE OF MAMMOTH SHIRE SPORT HORSES SINCE YOU HAVEN'T RETURNED A SINGLE TEXT OF MINE. LOVE, MOM

TEXT TO MOM

HAY, MOM, WHY'D YOU BALE? SORRY I DIDN'T CALL YOU BACK. I'VE BEEN FEELING A LITTLE HORSE. I GOTTA TROT OFF. SOCCER MATCH TODAY.

GIDDY-UP.

JACKPOT

MISS QUATTLEBAUM FINALLY PAIRS YOU WITH APRIL FOR THE WALTZ, WHICH IS SENSATIONAL, **AND**

ONE-TWO-THREE...

BECAUSE THE RIGHT HAND MUST GUIDE THE SMALL OF **MILADY'S** BACK

TWO-TWO-THREE...

ACROSS THE GLOSSY HARDWOOD WHILE THE LUCKY LEFT

THREE-TWO-THREE...

GETS TO HOLD HER HAND, TWIRL HER OUT.

FOUR-TWO-THREE...

SPIN HER IN, PULL HER CLOSE, NOSE TO NOSE, FOR THE LONGEST, MOST AWESOME SIX SECONDS EVER, DURING WHICH YOU QUIETLY WISH THAT THE GERMAN DANCER WHO INVENTED THE WALTZ HAD INCLUDED A **KISS**.

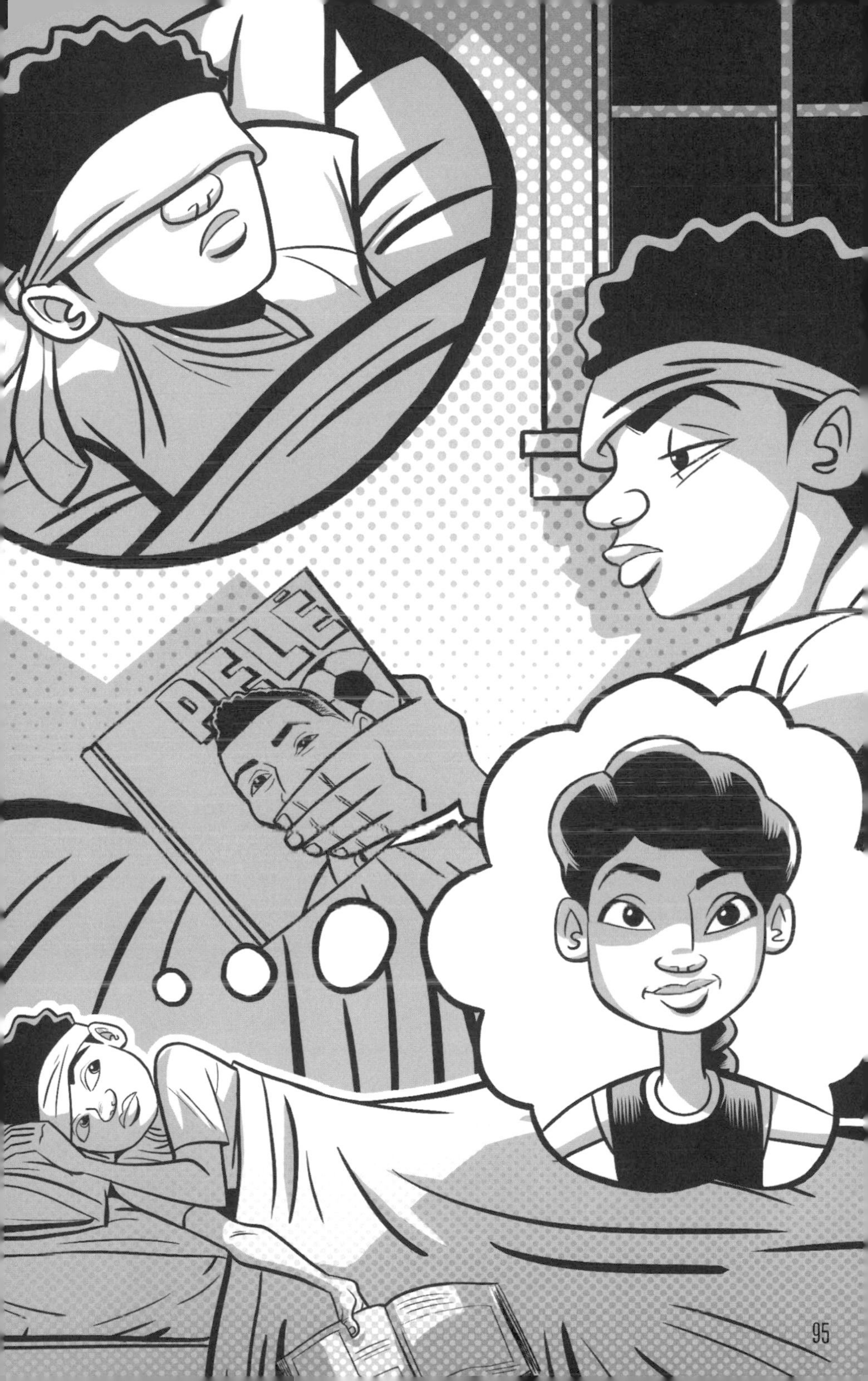
PELÉ

STANDING IN THE LUNCH LINE

COBY SAYS, JUST ASK YOUR DAD TO TAKE US TO SCHOOL. DANG!

TRUST ME, YOU DON'T WANT THAT. HE'S GOT LOGORRHEA,* YOU ANSWER.

THAT SOUNDS DISGUSTING. IT IS.

HEY, NICK, THERE'S APRIL. GO FOR IT.

NAH, I'M GOOD.

DEAN AND **DON** AREN'T EVEN AROUND. STOP BEING SCARED.

I'M NOT. I JUST DON'T FEEL LIKE IT TODAY.

HEY, APRIL!

HE SCREAMS, THEN DUCKS. SHE TURNS AND LOOKS. AT **ME**.

> *LOGORRHEA [LOG-UH-REE-UH] NOUN: AN EXCESSIVE USE OF WORDS. IF I HAD A MILLION DOLLARS, I'D INVEST ALL OF MY MONEY TO CURE THIS DISEASE.

BIG TROUBLE

YOU WALK UP TO APRIL,
SCARED STRAIGHT.

WHEN'S YOUR NEXT GAME?
SHE ASKS.

I'M COMING WITH CHARLENE
AND MY COUSIN. SCORE A GOAL
FOR ME, SHE SAYS, THEN SHOOTS
A **SMILE**.

BUMP!

WHY'D YOU DO THAT, **DON**? APRIL SNAPS AS YOU PICK UP THE **FOOD**.

NOBODY'S TALKING TO YOU, **APE**.

SHUT UP, SHE FIRES BACK, AND GIVES HIM A SHOVE THAT ONLY MAKES HIM LAUGH MORE,

AND MAKES YOU **WANNA. SHUT. HIM. UP.**

STAND UP

HER NAME'S APRIL, YOU SAY WITH A MEAN SCOWL. HOW'D YOU LIKE IT IF I CALLED YOU **DAW** INSTEAD OF **DON**.

DAW? HE SAYS, LAUGHING LOUD ENOUGH TO STARTLE THE FEW KIDS IN THE LUNCHROOM WHO WEREN'T PAYING ATTENTION.

THAT DOESN'T EVEN MAKE SENSE.

DAW IS THE ORIGIN OF YOUR NAME, YOU CONTINUE. IT MEANS SIMPLETON, AS IN **IDIOT**.

HE STOPS LAUGHING.

AS FOR YOUR LAST NAME, EGGLESTON, WELL, THAT COMES FROM
THE LATIN WORD EGESTA, AS IN EXCREMENT, OR DUNG.

SO MAYBE WE SHOULD CALL YOU DUMB DUNG. NOW THE WHOLE
LUNCHROOM IS CRACKING UP, APRIL TOO.

OR BETTER YET, HOW ABOUT STUPID CRAP! A GUY IN THE BACK OF THE
LINE HOLLERS, SHOTS FIRED!

EVEN THE BLOND-HAIRED
CAFETERIA LADY JOINS IN ON THE FUN:
OH MY, YOU JUST GOT COOKED, SON.

THE PLACE GOES CRAZY.

IT'S LIKE YOU'RE ABOUT TO SCORE AND
EVERYONE'S CHANTING YOUR NAME.

NICK HALL!
NICK HALL!
NICK HALL!

HE CHARGES, TRIES TO
TACKLE YOU.

AND THEN (WHAT THE—)

YOU SNAP OUT OF IT
AND REALIZE THAT NONE
OF THIS HAPPENED.

ARGGH!!

BACK TO LIFE

SAY SOMETHING, **PUNK**,
ONE-EYED **DEAN** SAYS,
STANDING IN FRONT OF YOU.

WAIT, WHERE'D HE COME FROM?

STAY AWAY FROM APRIL, HE
CONTINUES, SHE'S MINE.

I'M NOT YOURS, AND YOU CAN'T
TELL HIM TO STAY AWAY FROM
ME! APRIL SHOUTS BACK.

LET'S GO, NICK, SHE ADDS.

DEAN KNOCKS YOU INTO
THE FRUIT STAND.

YOU FALL. SO DO ALL THE
BANANAS AND APPLES.

A HAND REACHES DOWN TO PICK YOU UP.

LET'S BOUNCE, COBY SAYS.

THIS HAS NOTHING TO DO WITH YOU, **HALF**RICAN, DON SAYS TO HIM, THEN DAPS ONE-EYED DEAN, WHO ADDS, YEAH, YOU **BL**ASIAN, RICE-EATING—

BUT BEFORE HE CAN FINISH
COBY COVERS UP ONE EYE,
AND HOLLERS, YEAH, WELL,
I GOT MY **EYE** ON YOU, DEAN,
AND THE PLACE BREAKS OUT
IN **OOOOH**S AND **AAAAAH**S

WHEN ALL OF A SUDDEN,

DEAN AND DON BOTH
BUM-RUSH COBY, WHO
PUNCHES DON IN THE
STOMACH BEFORE
ONE-EYED DEAN KNOCKS
HIM TO THE **GROUND**.

YOU JUST, **GET THIS**, STAND THERE, STILL FROZEN WITH BUBBLE YUM STUCK IN YOUR THROAT AND KING CHOCOLATE

SQUISHED IN YOUR POCKET WHILE YOUR **BEST FRIEND**

TRIES TO FIGHT OFF TWO PISSED-OFF DOGS BY

HIMSELF.

DO-OVER

YOU KNOW HOW SOMETIMES AT NIGHT WHEN YOU CAN'T SLEEP AND YOU'RE WATCHING THE STARS GO ROUND AND ROUND ON THE CEILING FAN, REPLAYING THAT ONE LOUSY INCIDENT OVER AND OVER IN YOUR MIND, WISHING YOU'D DONE SOMETHING DIFFERENT AND THAT IF YOU HAD A **DO-OVER** YOU DEFINITELY WOULDA SWOOPED DOWN ON THEM JOKERS LIKE A VULTURE INSTEAD OF JUST CIRCLING ABOVE, STANDING IDLY BY WHILE YOUR BEST FRIEND GETS A **BLACK** EYE AND SUSPENDED FROM SCHOOL?

CONSEQUENCES

THE TWINS GET SENT BACK TO **ABC** FOR THE REST OF THE SCHOOL YEAR.

COBY GETS TWO DAYS' **SUSPENSION**.

YOU GET **NOTHING**.

FREE AS A **BIRD**.

THE DAY AFTER

THE FIGHT, PRINCIPAL MILLER SENDS A LETTER TO ALL PARENTS SAYING RACISM WILL NOT BE TOLERATED AT **LANGSTON HUGHES.**

THEN WE HAVE A **LOOONNNNNG** ASSEMBLY AND WATCH **MARTIN LUTHER KING'S**

"I HAVE A DREAM" SPEECH,

WHICH YOU KNOW BY HEART FROM LISTENING TO IT FIFTY-ELEVEN TIMES AT HOME.

CONVERSATION

I GOT AN EMAIL FROM PRINCIPAL MILLER.
EVERYONE GOT THAT.

I ALSO GOT A CALL.
...

RACISM IS SERIOUS, NICHOLAS.
I KNOW, DAD.

WERE THESE BOYS PICKING ON YOU?
IT'S NOTHING. I CAN HANDLE IT.

BY FIGHTING?
I WASN'T FIGHTING.

PRINCIPAL MILLER SAYS YOU WERE MIXED UP IN ALL THIS.
AND COBY GOT SUSPENDED? THAT'S NOT GOOD.
THEY STARTED IT.

SON, IF THEY'RE BULLYING YOU, I CAN SCHEDULE A MEETING
WITH THEIR PARENTS AND THE PRINCIPAL.

**DAD, NO. YOU DON'T UNDERSTAND. I'LL BE FINE.
CAN I GET BACK TO MY HOMEWORK NOW?**

THE LAST TIME YOU GOT INTO A FIGHT

THERE'S ONLY BEEN ONE FIGHT.

IT DIDN'T GO WELL.

HAPPENED IN FOURTH GRADE, DURING SOCIAL STUDIES.

SOME KID NAMED TRAVIS PUT HIS FINGERNAIL IN YOUR HAIR.

YOU KICKED HIS DESK.

HE DIDN'T LIKE THAT.

TOLD YOU TO MEET HIM AFTER SCHOOL ON THE PLAYGROUND.

YOU'D BEEN TAKING TAE KWON DO LESSONS, SO HE WAS IN FOR A

BEAT DOWN.

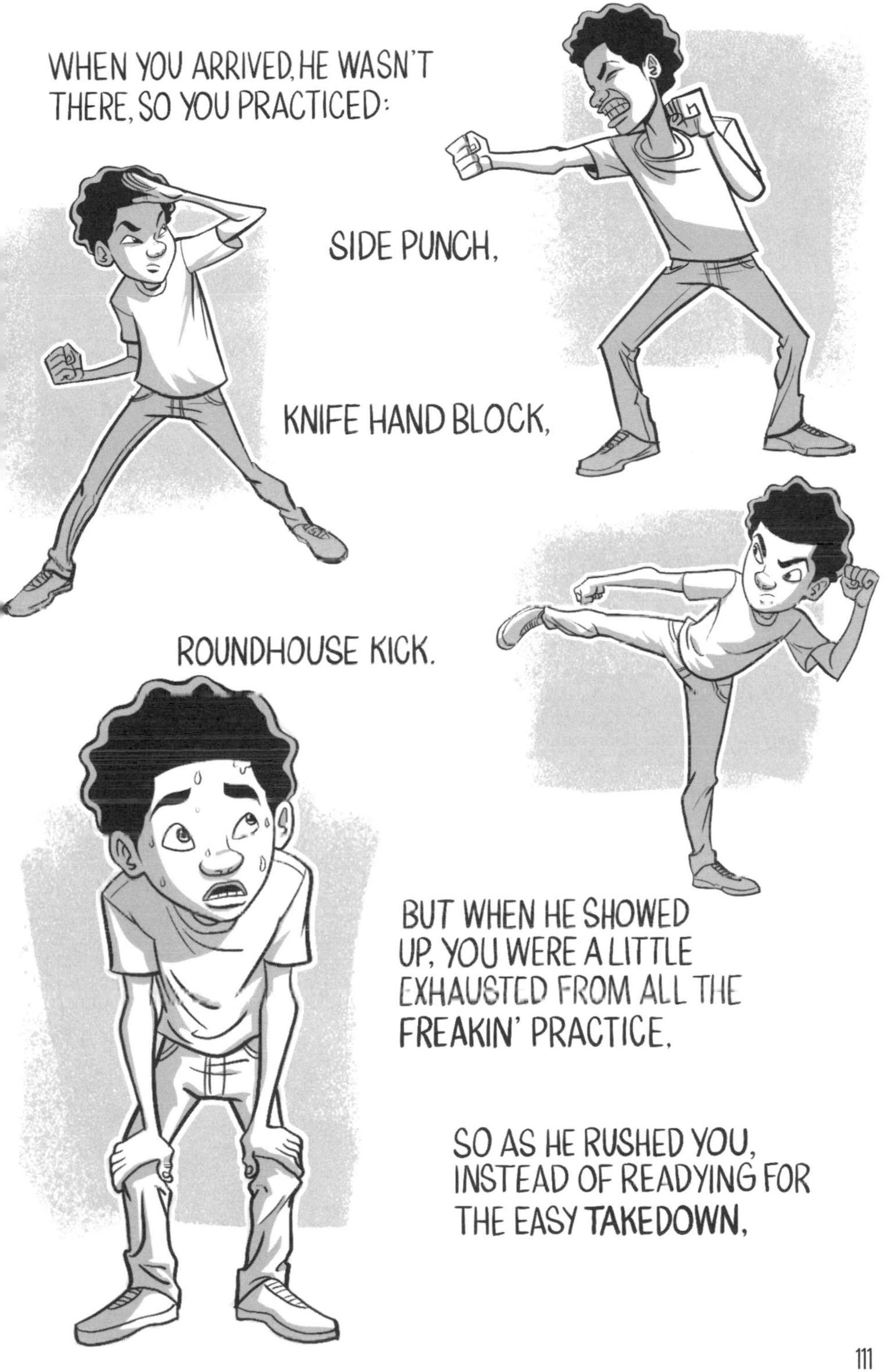
WHEN YOU ARRIVED, HE WASN'T THERE, SO YOU PRACTICED:
SIDE PUNCH,
KNIFE HAND BLOCK,
ROUNDHOUSE KICK.
BUT WHEN HE SHOWED UP, YOU WERE A LITTLE EXHAUSTED FROM ALL THE FREAKIN' PRACTICE.
SO AS HE RUSHED YOU, INSTEAD OF READYING FOR THE EASY **TAKEDOWN**,

YOU CALLED **TIME OUT**,
AND TURNED AROUND

FOR A BREATHER WHEN HE
JUMPED YOU FROM BEHIND,

AND YOU NEVER WENT
BACK TO **TAE KWON DO.**

LAST NIGHT YOU COULDN'T WATCH TV

BECAUSE DAD CANCELED THE CABLE, SO YOU MISSED THE WALKING DEAD.

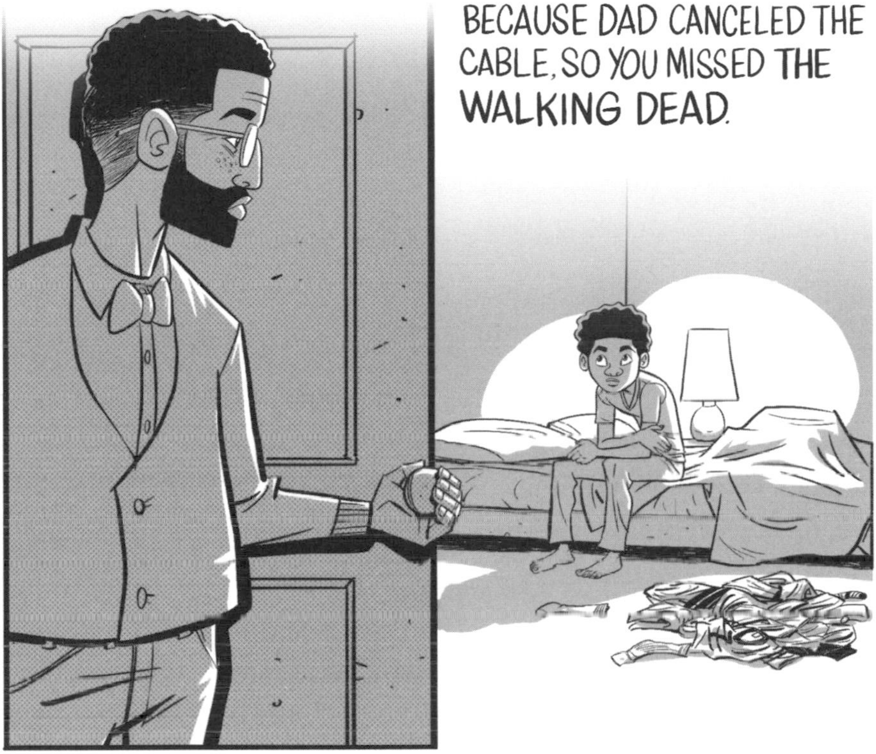

THIS MORNING HE TELLS YOU THAT YOU'RE NOT GETTING THIS WEEK'S ALLOWANCE 'CAUSE OF YOUR MOUNTAIN OF UNWASHED CLOTHES.

AND NOW MS. HARDWICK IS READING ANOTHER BORING BOOK IN CLASS.

AND APRIL HASN'T SMILED AT YOU SINCE THE LUNCHROOM BRAWL.

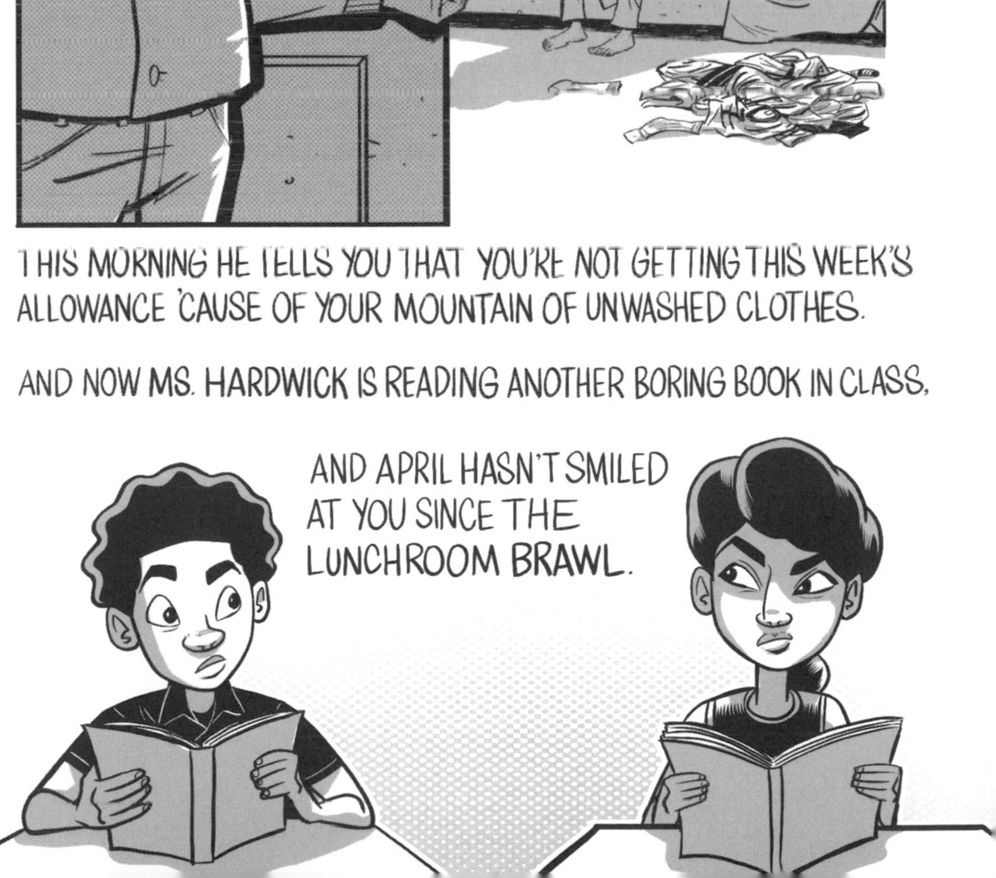

APRIL IS

LOVELY
INTELLIGENT
MAGNETIC
ELECTRIC
RED-HOT
EASYGOING
NICE
COURAGEOUS
ELEGANT

CAUGHT

THE INTENSITY ON YOUR FACE IS DEAFENING, NICHOLAS HALL!

WHAT? HUH?

IF ONLY YOU WERE CONCENTRATING AS MUCH ON **THE WATSONS GO TO BIRMINGHAM** AS YOU WERE ON THAT NOTEBOOK OF YOURS.

CARE TO SHOW US WHAT YOU'VE BEEN WORKING ON?

COME UP HERE. AND BRING YOUR NOTEBOOK WITH YOU.

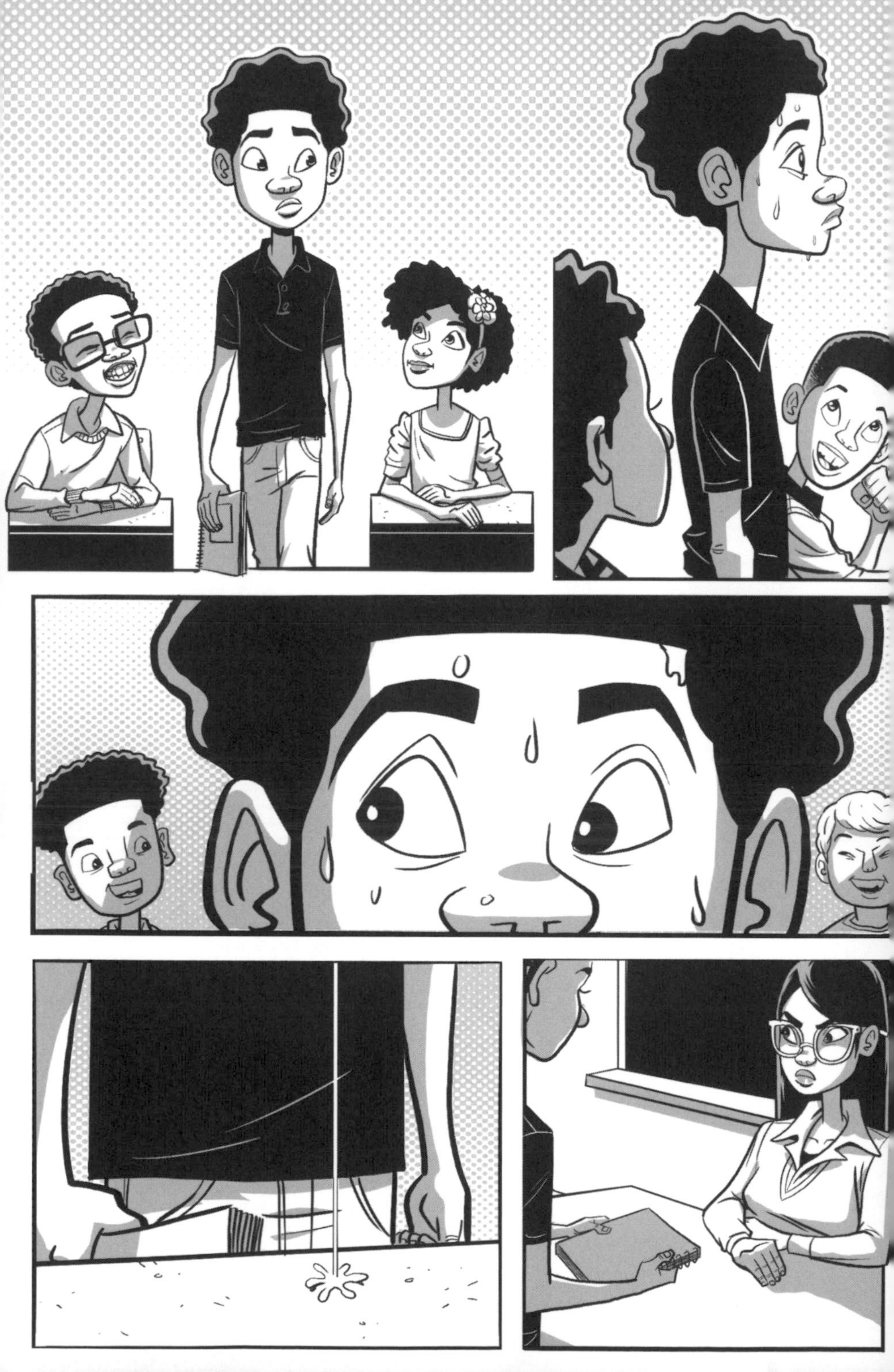

THEN SHE SMILES

IF THERE WERE AN AWARD FOR WORST TEACHER, MS. HARDWICK WOULD WIN HANDS DOWN. SHE'S HAD A FROWN ON HER FACE SINCE THE BEGINNING OF THE SCHOOL YEAR. SO, WHEN SHE SMILES, YOU'RE **FLUMMOXED.***

WELL, IT APPEARS THAT **NICHOLAS** HERE HAS BEEN DOING A LITTLE BIT OF EXTRA CREDIT, SHE SAYS, STARING AT YOUR **NOTEBOOK**.

NOW YOU'RE REALLY CONFUSED.

SHE HANDS YOU BACK YOUR NOTEBOOK. NICHOLAS, WOULD YOU PLEASE SHARE THIS LOVELY NEW VOCABULARY WORD YOU'VE DISCOVERED.

SHE WINKS AT YOU WHEN SHE SAYS LOVELY.

SHE'S GONNA EMBARRASS YOU IN FRONT OF EVERYONE. **DO I HAVE TO, MS. HARDWICK?**

IT'S SUCH A WONDERFUL, RHYTHMIC WORD. SPELL IT FOR THE CLASS PLEASE. YOU DO, AND THEN SHE GOES IN FOR THE KILL.

* FLUMMOXED [FLUHM-UHKST] VERB. TO BEWILDER OR CONFUSE. WHY IS HARDWICK SMILING?

DO YOU KNOW WHAT IT MEANS, NICHOLAS?
NO, YOU LIE. (WHY IS SHE STILL SMILING?)
LET'S GIVE NICHOLAS A
ROUND OF APPLAUSE.
EVERYONE DOES.

EVEN APRIL.

CLASS, YOUR HOMEWORK IS TO
DEFINE LIMERENCE AND USE IT
IN A SENTENCE.

WHEW, YOU THINK, AS YOU WALK BACK TO
YOUR SEAT.

(I SURVIVED!)

MS. HARDWICK ISN'T ALL THAT BAD.

YOU ESCAPED, BUT JUST BEFORE YOU SIT
DOWN WINNIFRED RAISES HER HAND AND
STARTS SPRAYING BULLETS
EVERYWHICHAWAY.

LIMERENCE

SHE SAYS, FROM THE FRENCH WORD **LIMIER**.

I CAN TELL YOU WHAT IT MEANS RIGHT NOW, MS. HARDWICK.

NOOOOOOOOOOOOOOOOOOOOOOOOOO!

GO RIGHT AHEAD, WINNIFRED.

LIMERENCE IS THE EXPERIENCE OF BEING IN LOVE WITH SOMEONE, COMMONLY KNOWN AS A CRUSH, BUT NOT ANY OLD CRUSH.

A. MAJOR. CRUSH

NICHOLAS B. HALL
BELOVED SON.
BEST FRIEND.
SOCCER STAR.
2003-2016 DIED OF ONOMATOPHOBIA.*
MAY HE REST IN PEACE.

*ONOMATOPHOBIA
[ON-UH-MAHT-UH-FOH-BEE-UH] NOUN:
FEAR OF HEARING A CERTAIN WORD.

DEAD!!!!!

COBY'S BACK

I SHOULD HAVE JUMPED IN, HELPED YOU IN THE FIGHT.
HE SHRUGS HIS SHOULDERS, TELLS YOU,
DON'T WORRY ABOUT IT, NICK. JUST HAVE MY BACK NEXT TIME.
DID YOU GET IN TROUBLE?

YEAH, I CAN'T PLAY IN ANY GAMES FOR A WEEK.
WHAT?! CAN YOU STILL GO TO DALLAS?

OF COURSE.
WHEW!

SORRY, COBY!
YEAH, JUST DEAL THE CARDS.

BLACKJACK IN THE LIBRARY

LET'S PLAY SOCCER AFTER SCHOOL, NICK.
I CAN'T.

GOT SOME CHORES TO
DO BEFORE MY
DAD GETS HOME.

YOU AND COBY

SIT ON THE FLOOR IN THE BACK NEAR THE BIOGRAPHIES, PLAYING CARDS, WHISPERING.

I ALREADY STARTED PACKING FOR **DALLAS**. YOU?

THINK SHE KNOWS?

EVERYONE KNOWS, NICK.

HOW? DID SHE SAY SOMETHING?

NOPE, BUT CHARLENE GAVE ME THIS NOTE TO GIVE TO YOU FROM APRIL.

SHHHHH! LET ME SEE THE NOTE.

WHAT NOTE? WHISPERS THE MAC, SURPRISING
BOTH OF US.
I TOLD YOU TO BE QUIET, COBY.

HEY, WHY ARE WE WHISPERING? WHISPERS THE MAC.
'CAUSE WE'RE IN THE LIBRARY, MR. MAC.

NOT IN THE DRAGONFLY CAFÉ.
WE DROP IT LIKE IT'S HOT HERE!
. . .

FELLAS, LET ME ASK YOU A QUESTION.
DO YOU HAVE A FAVE BOOK?

YEAH, A CHECKBOOK, YOU SAY.
GIVE ME SOME CASH.

GOOD ONE, NICK, COBY SAYS, LAUGHING
ALONG WITH YOU.

HA! HA! I'M TALKING ABOUT
A BOOK THAT WOWS YOU.
JUST TOTALLY RIPS YOUR HEART
OUT OF YOUR CHEST AND THEN
BRUTALLY STOMPS ON IT.

THAT KIND OF BOOK!

OH, WOW! YOU SAY.
WHEN YOU FIND THAT KIND OF BOOK, HOLLA AT US, MR. MAC.

HOW WAS THAT SOCCER BOOK I LOANED YOU, NICK?
UH, ABOUT THAT—IT'S A KIDS' BOOK, MR. MAC.

YEAH, BUT IT'S ABOUT PELÉ, HE SAYS.

REALLY, IT'S A BOOK ABOUT PELÉ, THE
KING OF FÚTBOL? COBY ASKS. I WOULD
READ THAT.

YOU WOULD?

NAH, PROBABLY NOT, BUT I'D DEFINITELY
LOOK AT THE PICTURES, COBY SAYS, AND
WE BOTH LAUGH.

OKAY, ENOUGH GOOFING OFF, FELLAS. AND HIDE THE NOTE YOU SLID UNDER YOUR LEG BEFORE MS. HARDWICK PEEPS IT.

BLACKJACK, COBY SAYS AS THE MAC WALKS OFF.

NOTE FROM APRIL

DEAR NICK, CHARLENE AND I THINK "LIMERENCE" IS BEAUTIFUL.

MEET ME AFTER MY SWIM CLASS.

CHANGE OF PLANS

COBY, YOU STILL WANNA PLAY SOCCER?

YEAH!

COOL!

BUT I THOUGHT YOU HAD CHORES? YOU'RE SUSPECT, BRO!

CONVERSATION WITH APRIL

NICE BIKE, NICK.
THANKS.

THANKS FOR COMING.
YEAH.

AREN'T YOU GONNA ASK ME HOW WAS SWIMMING CLASS?
HOW WAS SWIMMING CLASS?

WELL, MS. HARDWICK JUMPED IN THE POOL.
WHAT? NO FREAKIN' WAY!

YEAH, SHE WANTED TO **TEST** THE WATER. GET IT? TEST?
THAT'S FUNNY.

DID YOU HEAR SHE ISN'T COMING BACK NEXT YEAR?
SERIOUSLY?

YEP. SHE'S GOING TO ANOTHER
SCHOOL. IN TEXAS.
WOW! THAT'S COOL!

I LIKE HER.
**YEAH, SHE'S OKAY, I GUESS.
YOU LIE.**

HEY, I'M GOING TO TEXAS.
THAT'S NICE. FOR WHAT?

DALLAS CUP. IT'S A PRETTY PRESTIGIOUS SOCCER TOURNAMENT.
I LIKE WHEN YOU SAY WORDS LIKE THAT.

PRESTIGIOUS? THAT'S NOT REALLY A BIG WORD OR ANYTHING.
BUT YOU KNOW A LOT OF BIG WORDS?

YEAH, THANKS TO MY DAD, THE VERBOMANIAC, I HAVE TO READ HIS
DICTIONARY OF WEIRD WORDS.
WHAT LETTER ARE YOU ON?

I JUST FINISHED **Q&R**.
WOW! LIKE, WHAT KIND OF WORDS?

LIKE, UH, QUATTLEBAUM.
MISS QUATTLEBAUM?

YEP, HER NAME IS A PORTMANTEAU WORD, WHICH MEANS IT'S MADE UP OF
TWO DIFFERENT WORDS. HER NAME IS GERMAN. QUATTLE MEANS "FRUIT,"
AND BAUM MEANS "TREE."
SO SHE'S MISS FRUIT TREE.
SURE IS, BUT WE PROBABLY SHOULDN'T CALL HER THAT.

THAT'S FUNNY. WHAT ABOUT MY LAST NAME, FARROW?*
UH, I THINK IT MEANS "PRETTY" OR SOMETHING.

. . .

SO, DO YOU LIKE SOCCER?

NOT REALLY.
OH!

JUST KIDDING. I LIKE WATCHING YOU PLAY.
. . .

HEY, I'M SORRY ABOUT YOUR PARENTS.
HUH? I MEAN, WHAT DO YOU MEAN?

I SAW WHAT YOU POSTED ABOUT THEM RUINING YOUR LIFE.
OH, I WASN'T, I MEAN, THEY—

MY PARENTS TRIP OUT TOO. IT'S SO ANNOYING.
I'M OVER IT ANYWAY.

WELL THAT'S GOOD, 'CAUSE I DON'T WANT YOU TO LOSE YOUR
SMILE AGAIN.

. . .

HERE COMES MY MOM.
RAINCHECK ON A BIG HUG.
SEE YOU IN SCHOOL, NICK.

OKAY, UH, THANKS, UH,
BYE, **APRIL.**

* FARROW [FAIR-OH]
NOUN: A LITTER OF PIGS.
NO WAY WAS I TELLING
HER THAT SHE'S A PIG.

THE ONLY THING

BETTER THAN GETTING A HUG FROM APRIL IS THE **PROMISE** OF GETTING A **HUG** FROM HER.

BOY RIDES HIS BIKE

FROM THE COMMUNITY CENTER TO HIS HOME LIKE HE'S ALWAYS DONE, ONLY THIS TIME, BEFORE HE EVEN GETS A BLOCK AWAY, HE MEETS TROUBLE.

WHERE YOU GOING, NICK? ASKS DON, NOT REALLY CARING ABOUT AN ANSWER.

YEAH, DIDN'T THINK YOU'D SEE US AGAIN THIS YEAR, DID YOU? SAYS DEAN.

THE ONLY THING TO DO RIGHT NOW IS GALLOP LIKE A **THOROUGHBRED** AS FAST AS YOUR BIKE WILL POSSIBLY GO, AND RACE FOR YOUR LIFE.

SEEMS LIKE TO ME, YOU OWE US, SAYS DEAN.

FOR WHAT? YOU MANAGE TO ASK.

FOR GETTING US KICKED OUT OF SCHOOL, **PUNK.**

GIVE US YOUR BIKE.

UH, I CAN'T GIVE IT TO YOU. I'LL GET IN TROUBLE.

THEN I GUESS WE'LL KICK THE **CRAP** OUT OF YOU.

BOY RIDES HIS BIKE FROM THE COMMUNITY CENTER TO HIS HOME LIKE HE'S ALWAYS DONE, ONLY THIS TIME, BEFORE HE EVEN GETS A BLOCK AWAY, HE MEETS **TROUBLE** AND ENDS UP **WALKING**.

BREAKDOWN

AN HOUR LATER YOU TIPTOE UP THE STAIRS, TRY TO SNEAK PAST HIS ROOM BEFORE HE — (TOO LATE.)

NICHOLAS, COME HERE. VERY NEXT TIME YOU DISOBEY ME, THERE'LL BE NO DALLAS.

NOW DO WHAT YOU WERE SUPPOSED TO DO AND COME HOME AFTER SCHOOL EVERY DAY. AND GIVE ME YOUR PHONE.

IT'S NOT FAIR, IT'S JUST NOT FAIR!
YOU BETTER LOWER YOUR VOICE!
I HAD TO WALK ALL THE WAY HOME!
WHERE'S YOUR BUS PASS? IS YOUR LIP BLEEDING?
I RODE MY BIKE. I'M GOING TO BED.
I ASKED YOU A QUESTION. AND WHERE'S YOUR BIKE?
THEY TOOK IT.
WHO IS THEY?
AND WHY'D YOU LET THEM TAKE IT?

WHY ARE YOU ALWAYS BLAMING ME?
NO ONE'S BLAMING YOU. I'M JUST ASKING—
I'M TIRED OF THIS. YOU'RE ALWAY FUSSING AT ME FOR NOT READING YOUR STUPID DICTIONARY OR CLEANING UP MY ROOM.
YOU DON'T LET ME DO ANYTHING.
YOU TAKE MY PHONE, YOU TOOK MOM, AND NOW YOU WANT TO TAKE AWAY THE LAST GOOD THING IN MY FREAKIN' LIFE:
SOCCER.

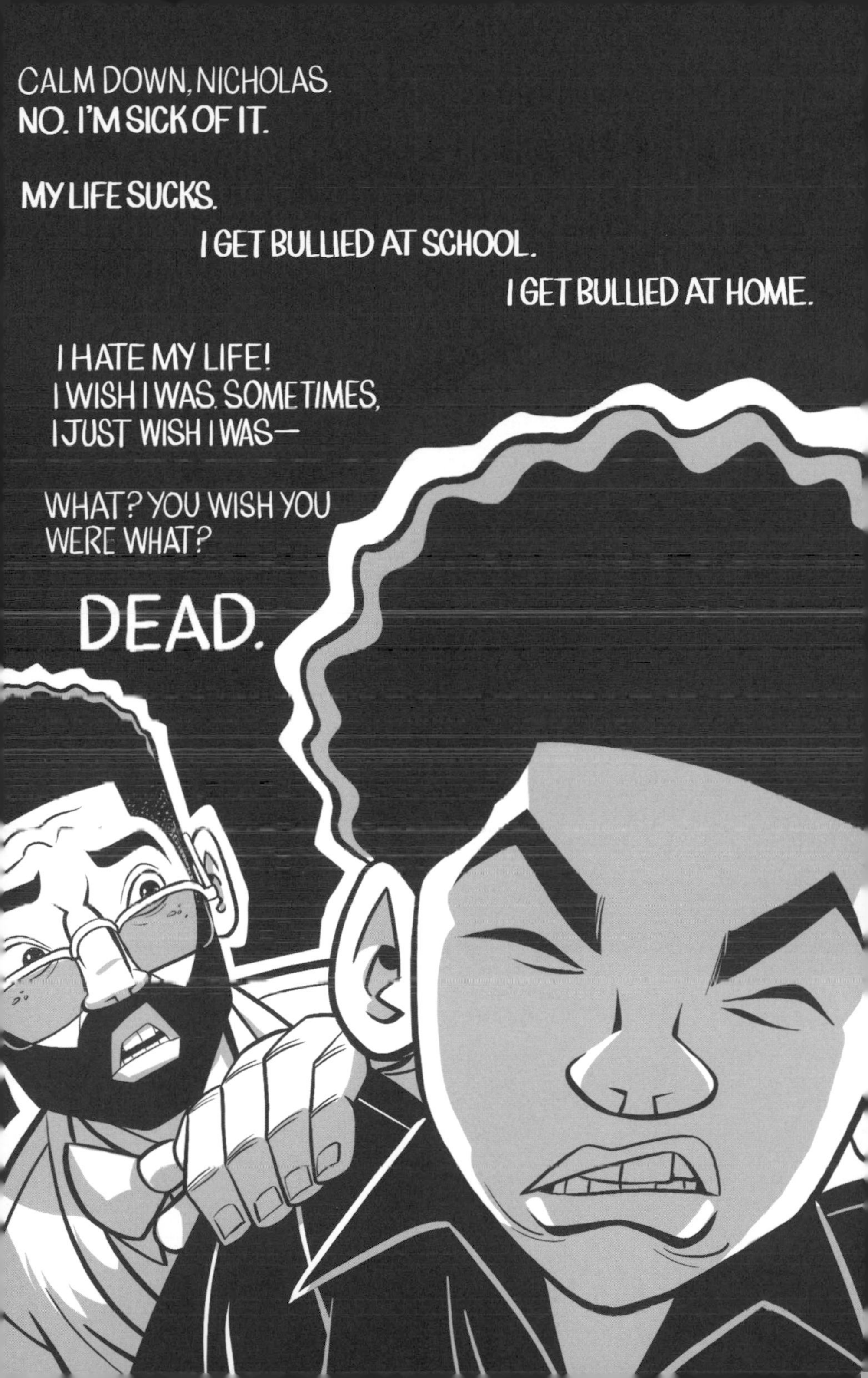

CALM DOWN, NICHOLAS.
NO. I'M SICK OF IT.
MY LIFE SUCKS.
I GET BULLIED AT SCHOOL.
I GET BULLIED AT HOME.
I HATE MY LIFE! I WISH I WAS. SOMETIMES, I JUST WISH I WAS—
WHAT? YOU WISH YOU WERE WHAT?
DEAD.

A GOOD CRY

THE BLASTING RAP MUSIC IN YOUR **HEADPHONES** MAKES YOU FEEL LESS SAD BUT STILL ANGRY ABOUT THINGS, SO YOU START RIPPING PAGES FROM BOOKS ON YOUR SHELF AND ONLY STOP WHEN YOU GET TO HIS DICTIONARY, BECAUSE EVEN THOUGH YOU'RE PISSED YOU'RE NOT STUPID.

AT THE TOP OF THE PAGE YOU ALMOST
RIPPED IS THE WORD SWEVEN*

YOU FALL ASLEEP REPEATING IT 497 TIMES
AND DREAM THAT...

* SWEVEN [SWEH-VUHN] NOUN: A
DREAM OR VISION IN YOUR SLEEP
THIS JUST MAY BE THE COOLEST-
SOUNDING (SWEVEN) WORD
YOU'VE EVER (SWEVEN) READ.

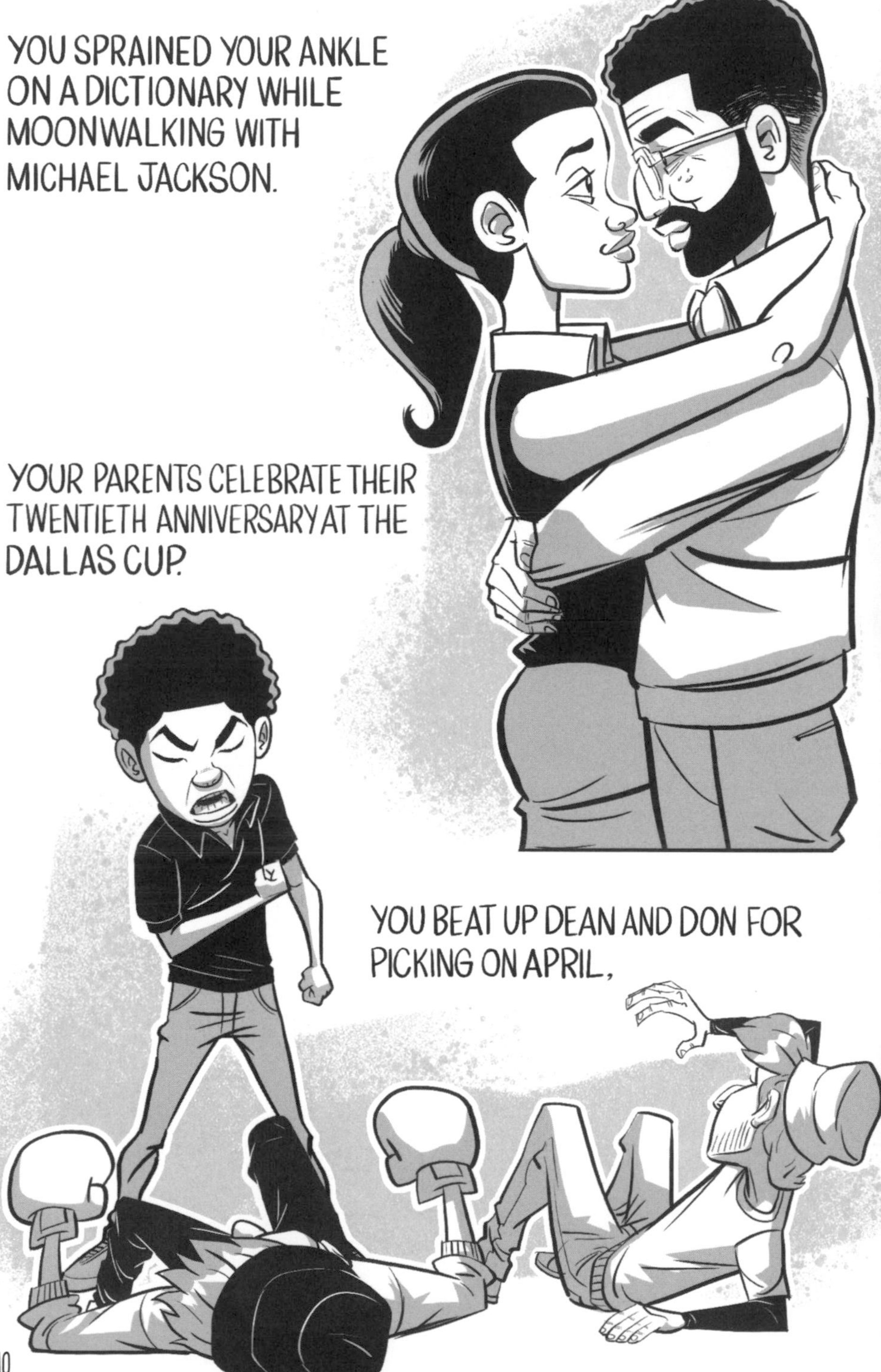
YOU SPRAINED YOUR ANKLE ON A DICTIONARY WHILE MOONWALKING WITH MICHAEL JACKSON.
YOUR PARENTS CELEBRATE THEIR TWENTIETH ANNIVERSARY AT THE DALLAS CUP.
YOU BEAT UP DEAN AND DON FOR PICKING ON APRIL,

AND THEN YOU FALL OFF A **MOUNTAIN**

BUT RIGHT BEFORE YOU
CRASH

YOU WAKE UP
CRYING IN YOUR
MOM'S ARMS.

WHAT ARE YOU DOING HERE?

DAD CALLED, SHE SAYS, WIPING YOUR TEARS. I DROVE ALL NIGHT.
WE'RE BOTH WORRIED ABOUT YOU, NICKY.
I'M FINE, MOM.

HE TOLD ME WHAT YOU SAID.
**MOM, OF COURSE I'M NOT GONNA KILL MYSELF. I WAS JUST UPSET
WHEN I SAID THAT.**

WHAT ABOUT THAT STUFF YOU POSTED ONLINE?
SERIOUSLY, MOM. I'M FINE. I SAY STUFF ALL THE TIME THAT I DON'T MEAN.

SO, YOU LIE?
C'MON, MOM.
...
...

LET'S GET OUT OF HERE.
HUH?

PUT ON YOUR CLOTHES. LET'S GO TO
THE FIELD.
I DON'T FEEL LIKE IT.

THAT'S A FIRST! C'MON, I'M GONNA
GIVE YOU A SOCCER
LESSON TODAY.
DO I HAVE TO?

YES, BUT CLEAN UP THIS
ROOM FIRST.

1 ON 1

LIKE LIGHTNING
YOU STRIKE
FAST AND FREE
LEGS ZOOM
DOWNFIELD
EYES FIXED
ON THE CHECKERED BALL
ON THE GOAL
TEN YARDS TO GO
CAN'T NOBODY STOP YOU

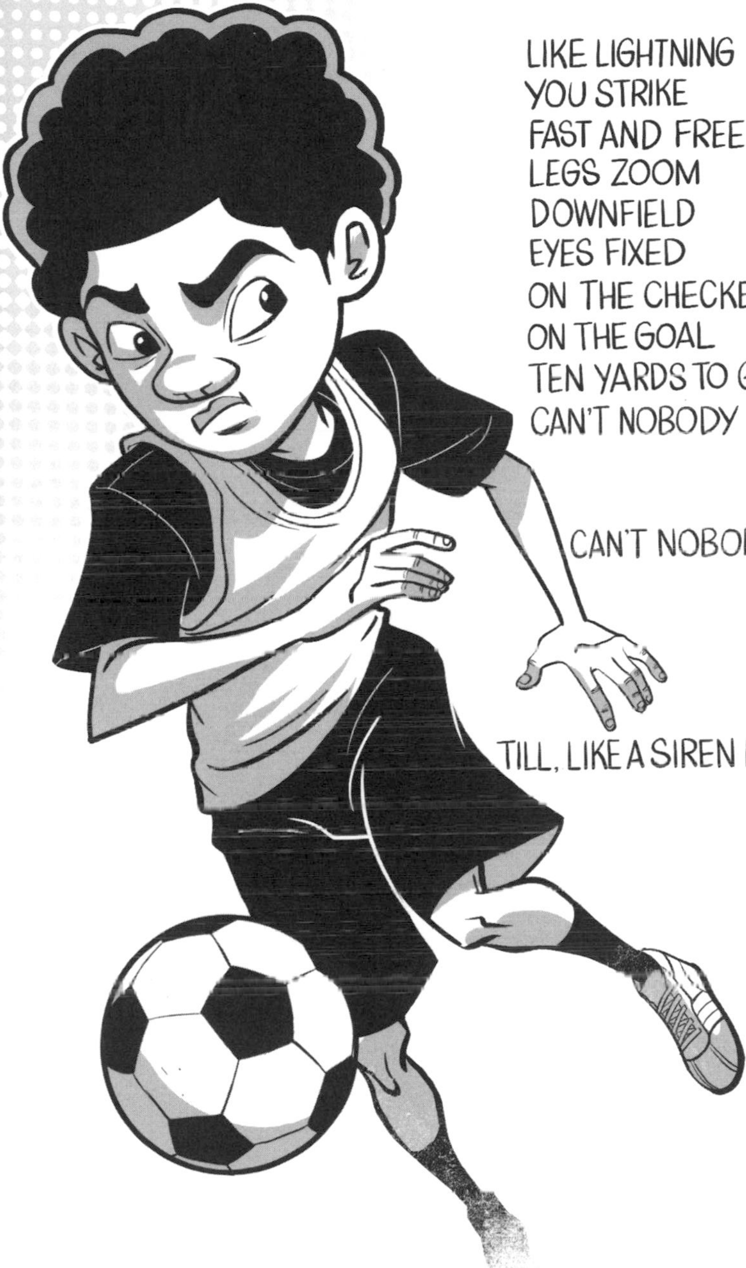

CAN'T NOBODY COP YOU

TILL, LIKE A SIREN IN A STORM,

SHE CATCHES YOU
ZIPS PAST YOU
STRIPS THE BALL
TRIPS YOU(FALL)
WATCHING HER
DRIBBLE AWAY
ALL THE WHILE THINKING
IT'S BAD THAT YOU GOT BEAT
BY ANOTHER GIRL
AND WORSE
THAT THE OTHER GIRL IS
YOUR MOTHER.

THIS MORNING
WAS JUST LIKE OLD TIMES: CINNAMON FRENCH TOAST, PANCAKES, PING-PONG.
YOU'RE FEELING A LITTLE BETTER UNTIL...

CONVERSATION WITH MOM

I'VE BEEN CALLING AND CALLING.
BEEN A LITTLE BUSY WITH—

SUGAR BALLS, NICKY! TOO BUSY TO RETURN A CALL?
I'M NOT A KID ANYMORE, MOM. I HAVE A LIFE.

OH, YOU HAVE A LIFE, DO YOU?
YEP.

DOES YOUR SO-CALLED LIFE INVOLVE THE LITTLE HOT MAMA
FROM DANCE CLASS?
HUH?

OH, REALLY, YOU'RE GOING TO PLAY CLUELESS.
NO, SHE'S JUST A FRIEND.

WHAT'S HER NAME?
APRIL.

THAT'S PRETTY. AREN'T YOU TOO YOUNG TO
HAVE A GIRLFRIEND?

**I DON'T HAVE A GIRLFRIEND.
PLUS, I'M ALMOST THIRTEEN.**

YOU'RE STILL MY
LITTLE NICKY.

**WHATEVER, MOM.
LET'S FINISH
PLAYING.**

YEAH, YOU CAN USE THE PRACTICE.
I'M GOOD, ACTUALLY. I SCORED TWO
GOALS IN MY LAST GAME.
YOU'D KNOW THAT IF YOU WERE HERE.

I HEARD THAT.
...
ARE YOU GIVING YOUR FATHER A HARD
TIME?
HE'S A JERK.

BE CAREFUL—HE'S YOUR FATHER.
AND SINCE WHEN IS MAKING
YOU DO YOUR CHORES BEING A JERK?

SO YOU TWO ARE TALKING AGAIN?

NICKY, HE'S DOING WHAT HE THINKS IS BEST FOR YOU.
MAKING ME READ THE DICTIONARY IS BEST FOR HIM, NOT ME.

YOUR FATHER LOVES YOU AND HE'S—
BLAH BLAH BLAH.

DON'T MAKE ME HURT YOU, BOY.
CAN WE JUST PLAY, PLEASE?

SO WE'RE OKAY?
YEAH, AS LONG AS YOU STOP
TRIPPING ME. THAT'S THE ONLY
WAY YOU SCORED A GOAL
ON ME TODAY.

YOU'RE THE ONE TRIPPIN'. THAT WAS NO FOUL.
MAYBE NOT WHEN YOU PLAYED IN THE OLDEN TIMES.

IF ONLY YOUR DEFENSE WAS AS GOOD
AS YOUR JOKES.
HOW LONG ARE YOU STAYING?

A FEW DAYS, BUT I'LL BE BACK IN TWO WEEKS.
YOU SHOULD COME TO MY GAME THIS WEEKEND.
WE'RE PLAYING IN NEW YORK, AGAINST THE
NUMBER ONE RANKED TEAM IN THE COUNTRY.

ABOUT THAT, NICK.

IT'S ONLY NEW YORK, MOM.
WE HAVE A TON OF CHAPERONES.

I'M AFRAID YOU WON'T BE GOING TO NEW YORK WITH THE TEAM.
YOU'RE GONNA DRIVE ME?

YOUR FATHER AND I HAVE DECIDED YOU WON'T BE PLAYING THIS WEEKEND. I'M SORRY.

WHAT?!

YOU CAN'T DO THAT!

DRESSED IN CAMOUFLAGE SNEAKS

THE MAC SEES YOU WALK IN
THE LIBRARY AND HOLLERS

(RIGHT IN FRONT OF
EVERYFREAKINGBODY):

IF YOU'RE LOOKING FOR
APRIL FARROW, YOU'RE
OUT OF LUCK.

NO BOOK CLUB
TODAY, **PELÉ**.

THEN HE WINKS AT YOU, LAUGHS,

GOES BACK TO SHELVING BOOKS
AND EATING HIS SANDWICH.

CONVERSATION WITH THE MAC

COWBOYS FAN? HE ASKS, SNEAKING UP WHILE YOU'RE ON THE COMPUTER. I SAW YOU GOOGLING DALLAS.

I'M GOING TO THE DR PEPPER DALLAS CUP. MY SOCCER TEAM GOT INVITED TO PLAY.

THIS WEEKEND?

IN THREE WEEKS. THIS WEEKEND BLOWS.

THE WEEKEND'S NOT EVEN HERE YET. THINK POSITIVE.

I HAD A SOCCER TOURNAMENT IN NEW YORK, BUT MY PARENTS SAID I CAN'T GO.

SORRY TO HEAR THAT, PELÉ. WHY DO PARENTS SUCK?

TRY A DIFFERENT WORD.

MY BAD, MR. MAC. WHY DO GUARDIANS SUCK?

HA! HA! WHO YOUR PARENTS ARE NOW IS NOT WHO THEY WERE OR WHO THEY WILL BE. YOU MAY NOT LIKE THEM NOW, BUT YOU WILL.

DOUBT IT!

YOU GET ONE CHANCE TO LOVE, TO BE LOVED, NICK. IF YOU'RE LUCKY, MAYBE TWO.

IT'S JUST HARD TO LOVE SOMEONE WHO CANCELS THE CABLE RIGHT BEFORE THE WALKING DEAD MARATHON.

SHRINK

INSTEAD OF PLAYING SOCCER IN THE BIG APPLE, TODAY YOU'RE SITTING IN THE CENTER FOR RELATIONAL RECOVERY ON A PLEATHER COUCH BETWEEN MOM AND DAD, STARING AT A QUOTE BY A MAN NAMED FREUD ON THE WALL BEHIND A,

GET THIS,

PSYCHOLOGIST WITH A BLACK AND WHITE BEARD LONGER THAN **SANTA CLAUS'S**, A RED PENCIL IN HIS MOUTH, AND A TENDENCY TO ASK STUPID QUESTIONS:

WHAT ELSE BESIDES SOCCER MAKES YOU HAPPY?

HOW DO YOU FEEL WHEN YOU'RE SAD?

DO YOU MISS YOUR MOM?

ALL BECAUSE YOUR BIKE GOT STOLEN AND YOU LOST YOUR COOL ONE NIGHT AND THEN POSTED THAT YOU NEEDED SOMEONE TO INTERVENE BETWEEN YOU AND THE MONSTERS AND YOUR COUSIN JULIE TOLD YOUR AUNT WHO CALLED YOUR DAD WHO TEXTED MOM WHO DROVE ALL NIGHT AND SCHEDULED AN APPOINTMENT WITH ST. NICK WHO THINKS YOUR POST WAS A CRY FOR HELP WHEN ACTUALLY YOU WERE JUST LISTENING TO EMINEM AND THOUGHT THE SONG WAS KINDA NICE.

YOU MISS

CINNAMON FRENCH TOAST WITH BLUEBERRY PRESERVES
HOMEMADE LUNCHES HER HEADLOCKS AND SLOPPY
KISSES HER SAYING SUGAR BALLS WHEN SHE'S PISSED
HER CHEERING AT MATCHES PING-PONG LATE SATURDAY
NIGHTS CLEAN CLOTHES ON SUNDAY DOUBLE FUDGE
MILKSHAKES AFTER CHURCH DINNER WITH REAL PLATES
AND GLASSES HER BAD HORSE JOKES AT THE TABLE BOTH
OF THEM HOLDING HANDS WATCHING TV FAMILY MEETINGS
AND, YES, YOU EVEN MISS THE GROUP HUG AFTER FAMILY
MEETINGS BUT, NO, NEITHER YOUR MOM NOR DAD IS A
MONSTER AND YOU DON'T NEED AN **INTERVENTIONIST.**

WHEN MOM STARTS CRYING, DAD TAKES HER OUT, LEAVING YOU ALONE WITH THE SHRINK

CAMOUFLAGING YOUR FEARS DOESN'T MAKE THEM
GO AWAY, NICHOLAS.
I'M AFRAID, OKAY. NOW WHAT?!

NOW WE TRY TO FIGURE OUT WHAT TO DO.
I KNOW WHAT TO DO. I NEED TO LEARN HOW TO FIGHT.

YOU THINK YOU NEED TO LEARN HOW TO FIGHT?
WHY ARE YOU REPEATING EVERYTHING?

THERE ARE WAYS TO DEAL WITH BULLIES.
LIKE WHAT?

WHAT DO YOU THINK ARE SOME
OF THE WAYS?

I GUESS IF I KNEW THAT
I WOULDN'T BE HERE.

DOCTOR FRAUD

WE HAVE FIVE MORE MINUTES REMAINING, NICHOLAS.

IS THERE ANYTHING YOU'D LIKE TO SAY TO YOUR PARENTS?

OTHER THAN IT KINDA BLOWS THAT I'M HERE INSTEAD OF PLAYING IN THE SOCCER TOURNAMENT, I'M GOOD.

. . .

REALLY, I'M FINE.

THE TWINS AREN'T COMING BACK TO SCHOOL THIS YEAR, AND I DIDN'T REALLY MEAN I WANTED TO BE DEAD.

I JUST... I JUST THINK... I GUESS I WAS MAD, AND IF THEY DON'T LOVE EACH OTHER ANYMORE, THEN THEY SHOULDN'T BE TOGETHER.

YOU ONLY GET ONE CHANCE TO LOVE, TO BE LOVED.

AND THEY LOST THEIRS.

I GET IT.

OF COURSE WE STILL LOVE EACH OTHER, DAD SAYS.
WE JUST CAN'T BE TOGETHER, MOM ADDS.

LET'S EXPLORE THAT, SAYS DR. SANTA. WHAT DO YOU THINK ABOUT WHAT YOUR PARENTS ARE SAYING, NICHOLAS?

I THINK BEING AN ADULT MUST BE CONFUSING AS HELL.

ALSO, I'M STARVING.
ARE WE DONE?

159

HOW DID WE GET HERE?

ON SECOND THOUGHT, THERE IS SOMETHING YOU'D LIKE TO ASK YOUR PARENTS.

ACCORDING TO A BROCHURE IN DR. FRAUD'S OFFICE, ADULTERY IS THE LEADING CAUSE OF DIVORCE AMONG AMERICANS. PRINCIPAL MILLER WOULD AGREE.

HIS WIFE GOT CAUGHT KISSING A MAN WHO WASN'T PRINCIPAL MILLER. **SPLITSVILLE.**

YOUR UNCLE JERRY QUIT HIS JOB AND YOUR AUNT JANICE FOUND OUT WHEN HER BRAND-NEW LEXUS GOT REPOSSESSED. SEPARATED.

COBY'S DAD AND MOM NEVER GOT DIVORCED BECAUSE THEY WERE NEVER MARRIED.

BUT YOU STILL DON'T KNOW WHAT HAPPENED

SO RIGHT AFTER THE FIRST BITE OF YOUR DINNER YOU SAY: **DAD, DID YOU CHEAT ON MOM OR SOMETHING?**

BEADS OF SWEAT CLING TO HIS FOREHEAD.

MOM STOPS CHEWING AND GULPS.

BUT BEFORE EITHER CAN ANSWER, GUESS WHO WALKS UP IN A T-SHIRT THAT SAYS:

I LIKE BIG BOOKS AND I CANNOT LIE?

INTRODUCTIONS

MOM AND DAD, THIS IS MR. MACDONALD, OUR LIBRARIAN.
DAD STANDS UP, SHAKES HIS HAND, AND THE MAC, IN,
GET THIS,
RED, WHITE, AND BLUE BOWLING SHOES, KISSES MOM'S HAND.

DAD KINDA FROWNS.
NICE TO MEET YOU TWO, FINALLY.
SORRY FOR THE SWEATY PALMS.
HAPPENS AFTER BOWLING.

MOM SLIPS HER HAND IN HER LAP (WHERE HER NAPKIN IS).
YOUR SON TALKS ABOUT YOU ALL THE TIME.
I HOPE NICE THINGS. MOM SAYS.

ACTUALLY, HE KINDA WANTS YOU TO TAKE IT EASY ON HIM.

LIFE AIN'T BEEN NO CRYSTAL STAIR FOR YOUNG
NICHOLAS HERE, HE ADDS.

THE SILENCE IS THICK AND SUPER UNCOMFORTABLE.

I'M JUST KIDDING, THE MAC SAYS, AND THEN BREAKS OUT
INTO A WAY-TOO-LOUD CHUCKLE.

WELL, I SHOULD GET BACK TO MY LADY FRIEND.
JUST WANTED TO SAY HELLO.

NICK, THEY'RE A LOT COOLER THAN YOU SAID,
HE PRETEND-WHISPERS TO YOU.

WELL, IT'S OUR PLEASURE, MR. MACDONALD, MOM SAYS.

OH, ONE MORE THING, NICK. DID YOU FINISH THAT **PELÉ** BOOK YET?

YOU LIE AND SAY YEAH, 'CAUSE THE LAST THING YOU NEED IS HE AND DAD GANGING UP ON YOU OVER A BOOK THAT'S NEVER GONNA GET READ.

HE TURNS TO LEAVE, AND YOUR MOUTH HITS THE TABLE WHEN YOU SEE

THE MAC'S **LADY FRIEND** IN RED HEELS WAVING FROM ACROSS THE ROOM IS MS. HARDWICK.

¡YUCK!

ALARM CLOCK

MOM, I OVERSLEPT, CAN YOU DRIVE ME TO SCHOOL, PLEASE? IT'S TOO LATE TO TAKE THE BUS.

SURE.

COOL?

HOW'D YOU GET TO SCHOOL?
MY MOM.

SHE'S BACK?
SHE WAS. BUT SHE'S GONE AGAIN.

WHY DIDN'T YOU CALL ME?
I OVERSLEPT.

DUDE, YOU NEVER OVERSLEEP.
I JUST WANTED TO SEE MY MOM A LITTLE LONGER.

YEAH, WHATEVER.
YOU WANT TO COME OVER AFTER SCHOOL?

DON'T YOU HAVE PRACTICE?
WE'RE JUST RUNNING TODAY.
COACH SAYS WE'RE READY.

READY TO GET DEMOLISHED LIKE
AN OLD APARTMENT BUILDING?
WE'LL SEE.

YOU SEE WHAT APRIL HAS ON TODAY? WHOA! BE BOLD, NICK!
YEAH, I SHOULD.

BE BOLD OR GO HOME.
I'M GONNA DO IT. I'M GONNA WEAR COOL TODAY.

HUH?
NO MORE CORDUROYS AND TURTLENECKS FOR NICK HALL.

WHAT ARE YOU TALKING ABOUT, NICK?
AT LUNCH, I'M ASKING APRIL TO BE MY GIRLFRIEND.

YEAH, RIGHT!
SERIOUSLY, I AM.

WHAT ARE YOU
GONNA SAY?
UH, WILL YOU BE
MY GIRLFRIEND?

THAT'S CORNY. BE COOL WITH IT.
HOW WOULD YOU KNOW? YOU'VE NEVER DONE THIS BEFORE.

YOU EITHER.
MY DAD GAVE MY MOM FLOWERS ONCE.

YOU GONNA GIVE HER FLOWERS?
I COULD, THERE'S SOME YELLOW ONES IN THE LIBRARY.

THOSE ARE FAKE, BRO.
OH! YEAH, YOU RIGHT. MAYBE I'M RUSHING IT.
SHE MAY NOT EVEN LIKE ME.

DIDN'T SHE ALREADY TELL YOU SHE LIKES YOU?
I'M JUST SAYING, MAYBE SHE DOESN'T LIKE ME ANYMORE.

DON'T CHICKEN OUT.
I ALMOST FORGOT. WE HAVE A SUB TODAY.

WHERE'S HARDWICK?
ALL THE ENGLISH TEACHERS ARE IN A MEETING TODAY.

COOL, WE CAN PLAY BLACKJACK.

DANG!

WHAT?
I FORGOT TO BRUSH MY TEETH TODAY.

SO.
I CAN'T TALK TO APRIL TODAY, LIKE THIS.

I GOT SOME GUM IN MY LOCKER.
I'LL JUST WAIT.

WHAT HAPPENED TO NO MORE CORDUROYS, CHICKEN?
I'LL WEAR JEANS ON MONDAY.

NOT COOL

AT LUNCH SHE WALKS BY, SMILES.

HEY, APRIL, COBY YELLS.

NICK HAS SOMETHING HE WANTS TO TELL YOU!

BAD

DON'T KNOW IF IT'S THE FISH NUGGETS YOU ATE, CHARLENE'S PERFUME, THE EGG SANDWICH SOMEONE'S EATING BEHIND YOU, OR COBY'S LEFTOVERS.

WHATEVER IT IS SENDS YOU RUNNING OUT OF THE CAFETERIA JUST AS THE VOLCANO OF BUTTERFLIES IN YOUR BELLY

AFTER SOCCER PRACTICE

GO WASH UP. I ORDERED PIZZA FOR DINNER.
NAH.

PINEAPPLE PEPPERONI.
UGH.

YOU'VE ALREADY EATEN?
GOT A STOMACHACHE.

DRINK SOME GINGER ALE. THAT'LL HELP.
IT JUST HURTS. I NEED TO LIE DOWN.

ARE YOU IN PAIN?
A LITTLE.

COME HERE, LET ME CHECK YOUR FOREHEAD.
REALLY? C'MON, DAD. I'M NOT A BABY.

YOU'RE HOT, NICK.
I JUST PRACTICED FOR TWO HOURS, DAD.
COURSE I'M HOT. GOOD NIGHT.

MAYBE YOU ATE SOMETHING BAD TODAY.
CAFETERIA FOOD IS ALWAYS BAD.
WE HAD FISH NUGGETS.
PRETTY NASTY.

I'M GONNA RUN OUT AND GET SOME ACTIVATED CHARCOAL.
CHARCOAL? LIKE FOR THE GRILL?

GO GET IN BED, NICK.
G'NIGHT.

IF YOU'RE SICK, YOU PROBABLY SHOULDN'T
PLAY TOMORROW.
OH, I'M PLAYING IN THE MATCH TOMORROW.

NICHOLAS—
DAD, I'LL BE FINE.

WE'LL SEE.

• • •

YOU WAKE UP AT FOUR A.M.

HUNGRY, SO YOU EAT. CHIPS. COKE.
THANK GOODNESS THAT'S OVER.

BORED, YOU EVEN READ THE PELÉ BOOK.

THE BIG MATCH

YOU AND COBY ARE ON TEAMS THAT LIKE EACH OTHER AS MUCH AS CROCS AND KENYAN WILDEBEESTS.

THERE'S ALWAYS A SKIRMISH DURING THE MATCHUP.

THERE'S NO BEEF BETWEEN YOU AND COBY, BUT YOU **WILL** GO HARD, COME WITH YOUR **A** GAME, 'CAUSE WHILE WINNING IS WICKED, BRAGGING ABOUT WINNING IS ICING ON THE STEAK.

GAME ON

YOU GOOD, NICK?
COBY ASKS AT MIDFIELD
FOR THE COIN FLIP.

GOOD ENOUGH TO
BEAT YOUR SORRY
TEAM, YOU ANSWER.

NOT GONNA HAPPEN!

PERNELL, YOUR CO-CAPTAIN,
JOGS UP.

COBY DAPS YOU, THEN
GOES TO SHAKE
PERNELL'S HAND, BUT
PERNELL LEAVES
COBY HANGIN'.

(TOLD YOU IT WAS
A RIVALRY.)

CALL IT, PERNELL
SAYS, THEN TOSSES
THE QUARTER.

COBY CALLS TAILS.

HE LOSES.

YOU CHOOSE THE BALL.

BEFORE COBY TURNS TO LEAVE, PERNELL CHIDES, SORRY ABOUT THAT, CHOPSTICK, THEN LAUGHS, BUT COBY LAUGHS BACK, THEN WINKS AT HIM, AND PERNELL IS **FLUMMOXED** OR PISSED **OR** BOTH.

BOTH TEAMS TAKE THEIR POSITIONS.

YOU KNOW COBY'S SMILE IS MISLEADING.

HE'S READY TO **POUNCE**.

SCORE

YOU PASS TO THE FORWARD, WHOSE SHOT STINGS LIKE WASABI, THEN

BOO-YAH!

RIGHT BEFORE HALFTIME

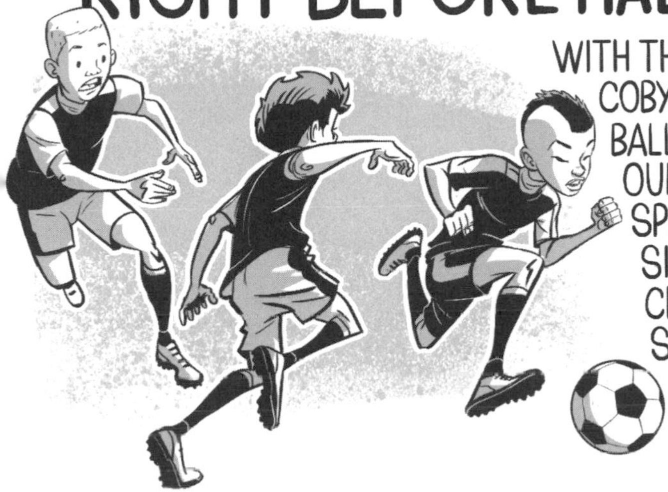

WITH THE SCORE 2–1, COBY DRIBBLES THE BALL PAST TWO OF OUR DEFENDERS, SPEEDS DOWN THE SIDELINES LIKE A CHEETAH, THEN SLANTS TOWARD THE MIDDLE.

PERNELL IS THE ONLY PLAYER FROM OUR TEAM LEFT BETWEEN HIM AND OUR GOALIE.

IT'S THE MATCHUP YOU KNOW COBY HAS BEEN ITCHING FOR SINCE THE START WHISTLE.

AS SOON AS PERNELL CHARGES COBY CUTS BACK AND YOU KNOW WHAT'S COMING NEXT.

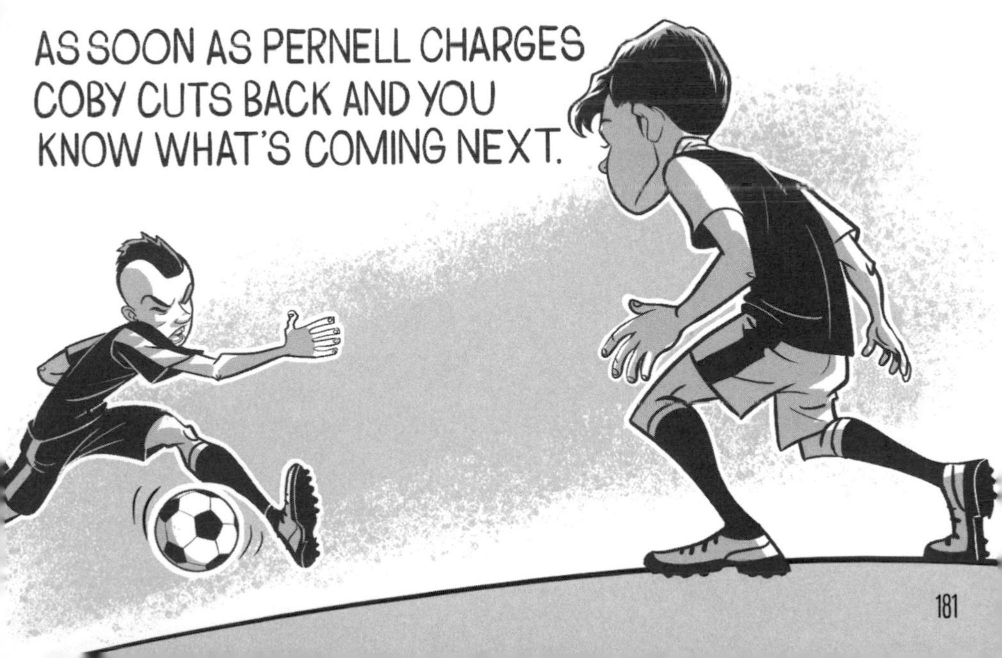

PERNELL DIVES IN
FOR THE TAKE...
OH, **WOW**!
COBY NUTMEGS* HIM.

*** NUTMEG** [NUHT-MEG] NOUN: A SOCCER TRICK IN WHICH THE BALL
IS DRIBBLED BETWEEN THE DEFENDER'S LEGS. IMAGINE A BALL OF
SUN SNEAKING THROUGH THE CLOUDS. LIONEL MESSI IS SO
GOOD HE COULD PROBABLY NUTMEG A MERMAID.
NOW THAT'S HOT.

HE DEMORALIZES PERNELL.
DROPS HIM TO HIS BUTT.
TREATS HIM LIKE A DOG.
SIT. STAY.
THE CROWD GOES WILD.
BOTH SIDES.
AND WHEN HE TIES THE GAME,
EVEN YOU GRIN AT YOUR BEST
FRIEND'S GENIUS.

PAYBACK IS A BEAST, ISN'T IT!

GUESS WHO'S BACK?

THE MAC IN ELECTRIC
BLUE CHUCK TAYLORS
RUNS OVER TO YOUR
BENCH DURING THE BREAK.

HEY, NICK. YOU DIDN'T TELL ME COBY WAS A BUS DRIVER.
HUH?

HE TOOK THAT FOOL TO SCHOOL. YOU WANT TO AGREE
LOUDLY BUT **THAT FOOL** IS YOUR TEAMMATE.
SO YOU JUST KINDA NOD.

YOU DON'T LOOK SO SWELL, PARTNER.
UH, IT'S JUST HOT OUT HERE (WHICH IS THE WORST THING YOU
COULD HAVE SAID, 'CAUSE THEN THE MAC STARTS RAPPING
"IT'S GETTIN' HOT IN HERE" IN FRONT OF THE ENTIRE TEAM).

183

HALFTIME

RIGHT AFTER YOU GLANCE AT APRIL WAVING FROM THE BLEACHERS, YOUR STOMACH **DETONATES**

KA-BOOM!

AND YOU LOSE IT RIGHT THERE BEHIND THE BENCH IN PERNELL'S GYM BAG.

COACH ASKS

NICK, YOU OKAY?
YEP, BETTER.

I NEED TO SUB YOU?
NO I'M GOOD, COACH.

GOOD! THEN GET IN THERE.

SECOND HALF

THE GAME'S TIED WHEN DAD
FINALLY SHOWS UP.

YOU THROW IN TO PERNELL,
WHO SCREENS IT.

YOUR BELLY'S IN A BOXING MATCH.

AND LOSING. BAD.

HERE COMES COBY.
PERNELL TAUNTS HIM,
FEINTS A PASS.

COBY DOESN'T FALL
FOR IT. INSTEAD HE
LEAPS LIKE A LION,

THEY COLLIDE.

PERNELL EATS DIRT, CURSES.
MAN AGAINST BOY, COBY SAYS.
STANDING OVER PERNELL.

THE REF HOLDS A YELLOW CARD TO A GRINNING COBY.
THIRTY-TWO MINUTES LEFT.

ARGGH!

NINE MINUTES LEFT. CAN'T THIS BE OVER ALREADY?

THE JABS TO YOUR BELLY ARE ALMOST UNBEARABLE.

DAD WAS RIGHT, FOOD POISONING.

YOU'LL NEVER EAT FISH AGAIN. **EVER!**

PERNELL'S DIRECT FREE KICK IS WIDE LEFT.

THE PAIN IS RIGHT BENEATH YOUR RIB.

PERNELL COMES OVER, GETS IN COBY'S FACE:

YOU THINK YOU'RE MESSI, PLAYER, BUT YOU'RE JUST DIRTY!

IF YOU WANNA PLAY DIRTY, WE CAN DO THAT, AND AFTER I TAKE YOU DOWN, I'M GONNA MAKE YOU WASH MY CLOTHES, CUT MY GRASS, LACE MY CLEATS.

YOU'RE ABOUT TO GET SHOOK, CROOK.

THE PAIN ONLY ALLOWS YOU TO LAUGH A LITTLE.

PERNELL IS CRAZY, BUT HE BETTER WATCH OUT, 'CAUSE COBY, WHO BUMPS PERNELL'S SHOULDER AS HE WALKS AWAY, LOOKS PRETTY FREAKIN' PISSED.

BOOKED

NO ONE IN FRONT OF YOU BUT
THE GOALKEEPER AND COBY.

YOU PASS IT TO PERNELL.
HE SHOOTS IT BACK TO YOU.

YOU GET READY TO DRIVE
THE BALL HOME.

EVERYTHING SLO-MOS
LIKE YOU'RE IN **THE MATRIX**...
AND COBY IS **NEO**.
AND **NEO** IS A BULL.
AND THE BULL'S-EYE IS ON YOU.
TWO CRAZED EYES GLUED TO THE BALL.
YOU WIND FOR THE KICK.

COBY'S CLEAT, AIMING FOR THE BALL,
FINDS YOUR —**THWACK!**—ANKLE INSTEAD.
THE TWO OF YOU FALL—**WHISTLE!** —SIDEWAYS, TO THE GROUND.

EEE-YOW!
YOUR ANKLE POPS!
YOUR STOMACH EXPLODES!

KNOCK.OUT.

ANKLE SPRAINS

ARE VERY COMMON IN SOCCER, SHE SAYS, TALKING FAST LIKE SHE'S
IN A HURRY TO SHOW YOU THE X-RAYS ON HER iPAD.

IT'LL HEAL PRETTY QUICKLY, A FEW DAYS.

COOL! YOU THINK, STILL IN A BOATLOAD OF PAIN.

BUT I'M AFRAID THAT'S THE GOOD NEWS.
THE BAD NEWS, YOU DON'T HAVE FOOD POISONING.

THAT SOUNDS LIKE GOOD NEWS
TO YOU.

YOU HAVE A PERFORATED APPENDIX AND WE NEED TO GET YOU INTO SURGERY.

WHAT DOES THAT MEAN? YOU ASK.

IT MEANS THAT YOUR APPENDIX, WHICH IS ABOUT THE SIZE OF YOUR TONGUE, AND LOCATED ON THE BOTTOM RIGHT SIDE OF YOUR ABDOMEN, HAS RUPTURED. THERE'S A TEAR IN IT, AND WE NEED TO SURGICALLY REMOVE IT BEFORE INFECTION SETS IN.

SURGERY?

WHEN?

NOW!

SURGERY

I DON'T WANT TO DIE, YOU SAY.

EVERYTHING'S GONNA BE FINE, NICK, DAD SAYS, ON THE WAY TO THE OPERATING ROOM.

MOM'S ON A FLIGHT, HE ADDS, SO SHE'LL BE HERE WHEN YOU GET OUT OF SURGERY.

IT'S A QUICK OPERATION, AND I'VE DONE A MILLION OF THESE, ADDS THE DOCTOR AS THE ORDERLIES ROLL YOU INTO THE ROOM.

YOU CLENCH YOUR FIST, AS IF THAT'S GONNA STOP THE OCEAN OF FEAR THAT'S GALLOPING TOWARD YOU.

COUNT BACKWARDS FROM TEN, ANOTHER DOCTOR SAYS,
AND BEFORE YOU COMPLETELY DROWN,
EVERYTHING GOES BLACK.

HOW ARE YOU FEELING, NICKY?

LIKE I JUST RAN A MARATHON, SWAM A FEW LAPS, AND PLAYED BACK-TO-BACK SOCCER MATCHES, IS HOW YOU ANSWER MOM'S QUESTION.

AND YOUR STOMACH? DAD ADDS.

LIKE BUTTER.
HUH?

SMOOTH AND EASY.
SMOOTH.

AND EASY, YOU SAY, GIGGLING, THEN DOZING BACK OFF TO SLEEP.

BAD

YOUR WHITE BLOOD CELL COUNT IS ELEVATED,
THE DOCTOR SAYS.

WHAT DOES THAT EVEN MEAN? YOU ASK, GRIMACING.

YOUR COUNT SHOULD BE NO HIGHER THAN FIVE THOUSAND.

WHAT IS IT? DAD ASKS, HOLDING MOM.
IT'S TWENTY THOUSAND. SO HE'LL NEED ANTIBIOTICS
TO FIGHT OFF ANY INFECTIONS.
HOW LONG DO I HAVE TO BE HERE?

WE WILL JUST NEED TO KEEP YOU FOR A FEW EXTRA
DAYS, BUT BY THEN THE WOUND SHOULD BE ALL HEALED
AND WE'LL SEND YOU ON YOUR WAY.

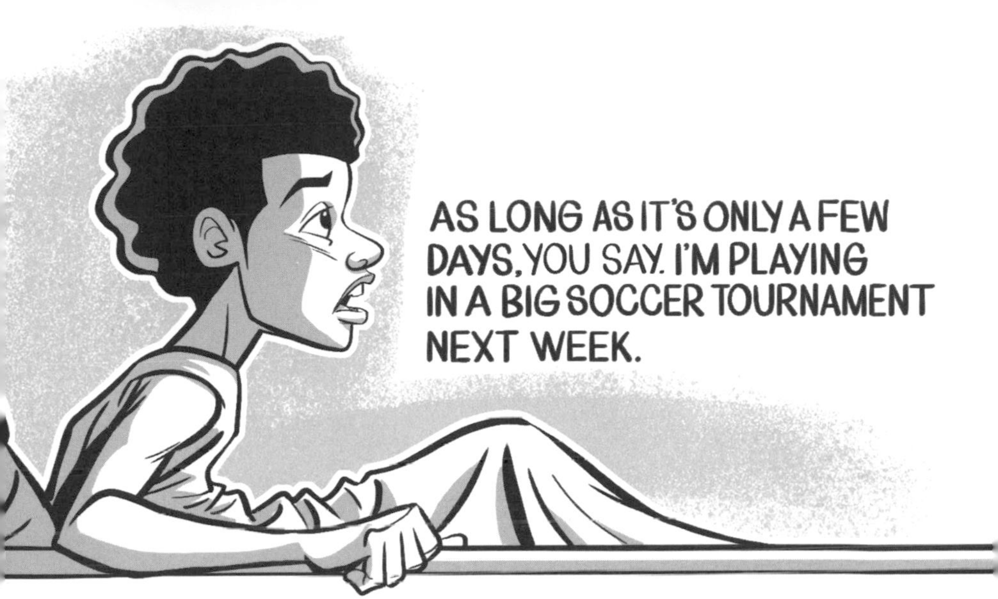
AS LONG AS IT'S ONLY A FEW DAYS, YOU SAY. I'M PLAYING IN A BIG SOCCER TOURNAMENT NEXT WEEK.

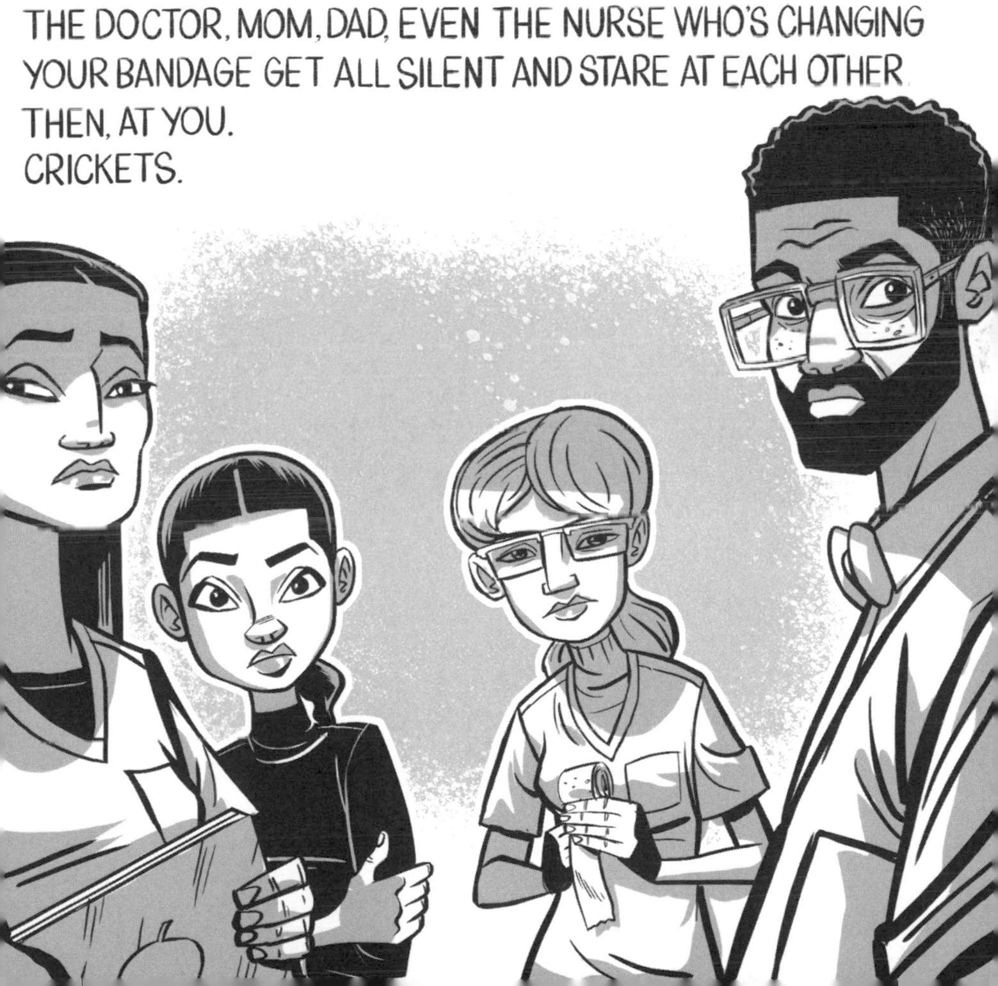
THE DOCTOR, MOM, DAD, EVEN THE NURSE WHO'S CHANGING YOUR BANDAGE GET ALL SILENT AND STARE AT EACH OTHER.
THEN, AT YOU.
CRICKETS.

WORSE

HE'LL BE OUT OF SCHOOL FOR A WEEK, OR TWO,
DEPENDING ON HOW HE FEELS, THE DOCTOR SAYS TO MOM,
WHO RESTS HER HAND ON YOUR HEART, WHICH BREAKS INTO
A THOUSAND LITTLE PIECES WHEN THE DOCTOR ADDS,
YOU'LL BE BACK PLAYING SOCCER IN NO TIME, NICHOLAS.

THE DALLAS CUP IS NEXT WEEK, YOU TELL HER.
HOW LONG IS NO TIME?
ONLY THREE WEEKS.

ONLY

ONLY. THREE. WEEKS.
BUT DALLAS IS IN ONE.
ONLY YOUR STOMACH IS SHATTERED AND YOUR
DREAM'S UNDONE.
ONLY NOT PLAYING SOCCER
MAKES THE PAIN SEEM SEVERE.
ONLY YOUR EYES CAN'T CONCEAL
TEAR AFTER TEAR.
ONLY YOUR SHIP IS SINKING
AND YOU'LL MISS ALL THE FUN.
ONLY. THREE. WEEKS.
BUT DALLAS IS IN ONE.

THE END

WHEN A HORSE BREAKS ITS LEG, THE BONE SHATTERS THE NERVES, THE LIVING TISSUE CAN'T HEAL 'CAUSE THERE'S NOT ENOUGH BLOOD SUPPLY.

THERE IS NO RECOVERY FROM THAT TYPE OF DAMAGE.

IT'S OVER.

THEY MAY AS WELL PUT YOU DOWN.

TV THERAPY

MERCY GENERAL HAS SIX ESPN CHANNELS, BUT THIS DOES NOT IMPRESS YOUR DAD.

THIS SUCKS

TOTTENHAM IS PLAYING ARSENAL BUT YOU SWITCH TO **HAWAII FIVE-O**, 'CAUSE WATCHING FÚTBOL WILL ONLY IRRITATE YOU, REMIND YOU OF WHAT YOU'RE MISSING.

ROOM SERVICE BRINGS YOU COLD SOUP, AND JUST BEFORE STEVE'S MOTHER'S MURDERER IS REVEALED, DAD TURNS IT OFF.

UNCOOL, DAD, YOU SAY.
YOU'RE NOT GOING TO BINGE ON COP SHOWS OR ESPN ALL DAY, HE SAYS.

DAD, THE BOREDOM IS KILLING ME.

MAYBE YOU SHOULD READ, HE ADDS, AND HANDS HIS DICTIONARY TO YOU.

NEW RULES

YOU GET FIVE TV MINUTES FOR EACH PAGE READ.

DOES IT HAVE TO BE YOUR BOOK? IT DOES NOT.

MOM KISSES YOU GOODBYE

SLEEP TIGHT, NICKY, SHE SAYS, AND THEY BOTH WALK OUT. HE STOPS AT THE DOOR, TURNS AROUND, LIKE HE FORGOT SOMETHING, AND JUST STARES AT YOU.

BOOKS ARE FUN, NICHOLAS, HE SAYS. THEY'RE LIKE AMUSEMENT PARKS FOR READERS.

YEAH, WELL, MAYBE THEY WOULD BE FUN IF I GOT TO PICK THE RIDES SOMETIMES, YOU ANSWER, YOUR EYES GLUED TO THE **W**s.

THE NEXT MORNING

THE NURSE ASKS IF SHE CAN GET YOU ANYTHING.

BACON, EGGS, AND FRENCH FRIES, PLEASE, YOU REPLY.

BREAKFAST

THIRTY MINUTES LATER, SHE RETURNS WITH BUTTERED WHEAT TOAST, CHERRY YOGURT, AND COBY.

CONVERSATION WITH COBY

HEY, NICK. WHAT'S UP?
THE SKY.

I SAW YOUR MOM AND DAD IN THE LOBBY.
YEAH, THEY NEVER LEAVE. IT'S ANNOYING.

I THINK THEY WERE ARGUING.
WHY YOU SAY THAT?

'CAUSE YOUR MOM WASN'T TALKING. AND YOUR DAD DIDN'T LOOK HAPPY.
HE NEVER LOOKS HAPPY.

TRUE. I WAS GONNA COME EARLIER, BUT MY MOM SAID YOU NEEDED YOUR REST.
WHAT I NEED IS SOME REAL FOOD.

TRUE.
PERNELL'S AN IDIOT. I SHOULDA DONE SOMETHING.

. . .

. . .

SORRY ABOUT THAT TACKLE. I WAS GOING FOR THE BALL.
YEAH, I KNOW. I WOULDA SCORED. WE WOULDA WON.

I DON'T THINK SO.
YOU GOT BOOKED?

YEAH, REF THREW ME OUT.
SORRY ABOUT THAT.

HOW'S THE STOMACH?
**IT'S FEELING BETTER.
THE FOOD'S DISGUSTING.**

THAT SUCKS.
YEAH... HOW'D YOU GET HERE?

MY DAD.
REALLY?

YEAH. HE'S COMING TO THE DALLAS CUP.
...

SORRY YOU CAN'T COME, NICK.
GOOD LUCK.

I'LL BRING YOU SOMETHING BACK.
BRING ME A JERSEY OR A BALL.

I'LL GET MY DAD TO BUY US SOME SWAG.
DEFINITELY.
COBY, YOU MISS HIM A LOT?

NOT REALLY. WE TALK ALL THE TIME, AND I SEE HIM
EVERY SUMMER.
OH.

I KNOW IT'S KINDA HARD RIGHT NOW, BUT YOU'LL GET
USED TO IT.
. . .

HEY, MAN U IS PLAYING ARSENAL. LET'S WATCH.
CAN'T.

HUH?
CAN'T WATCH TV, UH, RIGHT NOW.

DEAR SKIP

MAC

YOU CAN FIND ME HERE—
I'M IMPRISONED, TRAPPED BY A VERBOMANIAC AND
LOCKED FAR FROM FUN, FROM FREEDOM.

WILL YOU **PLEASE** BUST ME OUT?

SAVE ME FROM THIS MADHOUSE OF
BOREDOM AND WEIRD WORDS.

BRING A DECENT BOOK ASAP.

P.S. PLEASE MAKE IT A THIN BOOK
WITH A LOT OF WHITE SPACE ON
THE PAGE. THANKS.

VISITORS' DAY

WHILE YOU'RE FIGURING OUT THE MATH OF IT ALL:
(TWO MORE DAYS IN THE HOSPITAL.
PROBABLY WATCH **8** TO **10** HOURS OF TV A DAY.
FOR A TOTAL OF **1,000** TO **1,200** MINUTES.
WHICH MEANS YOU HAVE TO READ AT LEAST
200 PAGES.

ARGGH!)

GUESS WHO STROLLS IN?

HELLO, NICHOLAS

MS. HARDWICK?
THIS ISN'T A PIGMENT OF YOUR IMAGINATION?

A MALAPROPISM, I REMEMBER.
VERY GOOD. HOW ARE YOU FEELING?

I'M CURED, I GUESS, BUT I CAN'T PLAY SOCCER.
I'M SORRY TO HEAR THAT. I DIDN'T HAVE APPENDICITIS, BUT I HAD KIDNEY STONES.

IT'S WORSE. NOT FUN. NOT FUN AT ALL.
WE MISS YOU IN CLASS.

WHO IS WE?
SINCE YOU'RE GONNA BE OUT FOR A FEW WEEKS,
I THOUGHT I'D BRING AN ASSIGNMENT.

... (YAY ME!)
MR. MACDONALD SAID YOU ASKED FOR A BOOK,
AND IT JUST SO HAPPENS, WE RECENTLY STARTED
A NEW ONE.

THE MAC IS A TRAITOR, YOU THINK.

HE COULDN'T MAKE IT TODAY, BUT HE WILL STOP BY TOMORROW, SHE SAYS, HANDING YOU A BOOK CALLED **ALL THE BROKEN PIECES.**

I THINK YOU MAY FIND A GOOD READ HERE, NICHOLAS.

THANK YOU, MS. HARDWICK.
I'M TAKING A LOT OF ANTIBIOTIC MEDICATION, YOU KNOW, SO I FALL ASLEEP A LOT, SO I'M NOT SURE HOW LONG IT WILL TAKE ME TO READ THIS, YOU SAY, YAWNING LOUD SO SHE CAN HEAR YOU.

ALWAYS THE COMEDIAN.

NICHOLAS, I BROUGHT SOMEONE TO SEE YOU. ARE YOU UP TO ANOTHER VISITOR, OR ARE YOU TOO SLEEPY? SHE SAYS, WITH A SMIRK.

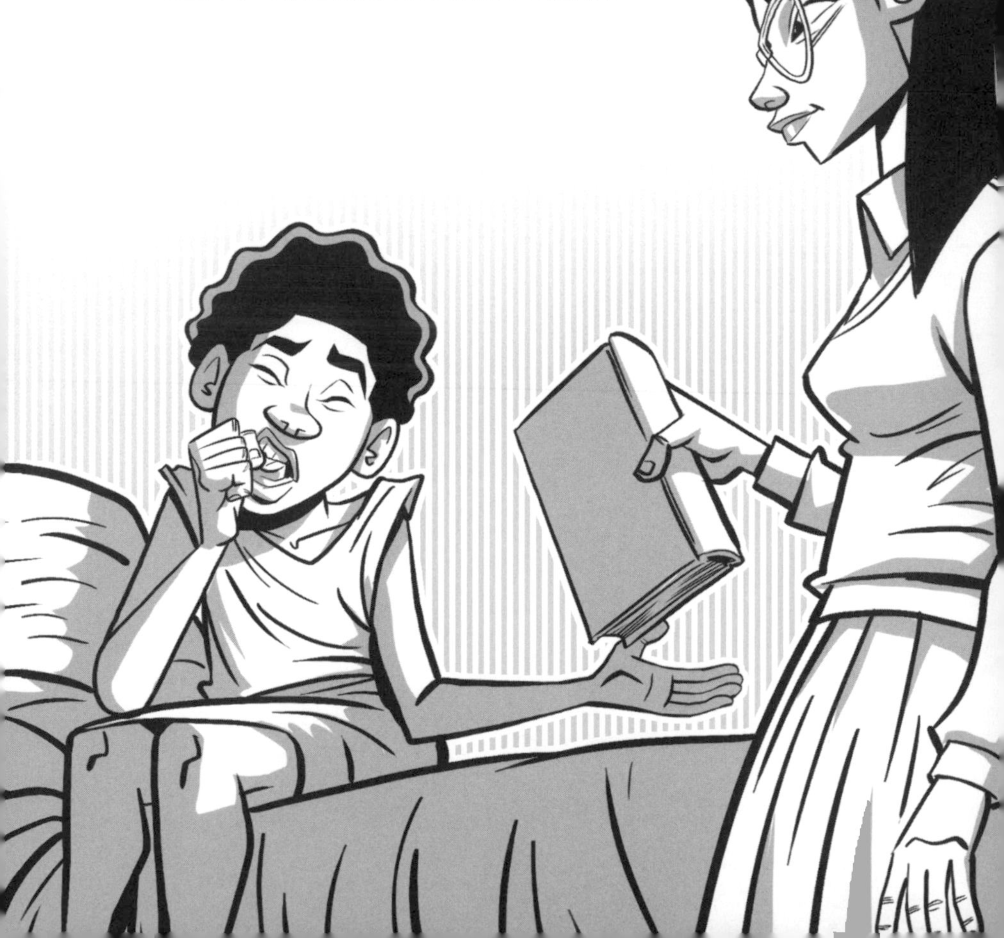

YOU GLANCE OUT OF THE WINDOW, WONDERING WHO IT IS.

IT'S PROBABLY MR. MAC, TRYING TO MAKE AN ENTRANCE.

SURE, YOU ANSWER.

WELL, THEN, YOU HAVE A GRAND DAY, AND A SPEEDY RECOVERY.

I MISS MY WORDSMITH, SHE SAYS, WINKING.

YOU OPEN THE BOOK, NOTICE THE NUMBER OF PAGES, **240**.

WELL, THAT'S PROMISING, YOU THINK, AS YOUR NEXT GUEST SAUNTERS INTO THE HOSPITAL ROOM.

HEY, NICK.

THIS **HAS** GOT TO BE A SWEVEN.

GOT. TO. BE. A. **SWEVEN.**

THERE IS NO WAY THIS IS HAPPENING.

YOU MUST BE DAYDREAMING AGAIN.

NO FREAKIN' WAY.

HI, NICK.

UH, HI, I'M, UM, APRIL. SORRY, I'M JUST A LITTLE STUP-ID. I MEAN—

(AND, OF COURSE, YOU MEAN STUPEFIED,* BUT YOU'RE TOO STUPEFIED TO ACTUALLY SAY IT.)

SORRY ABOUT YOUR APPENDIX.
THE WHOLE CLASS SIGNED THIS.

SHE HANDS YOU A GET-WELL CARD SIGNED BY EVERYBODY.

I'M SORRY YOU CAN'T PLAY SOCCER.

THAT MUST MAKE YOU FEEL PRETTY, UH, IRASCENT.

YOU SHOOT HER A LOOK OF SURPRISE.

WHAT?! IT MEANS ANGRY.
I KNOW WHAT IT MEANS.

* STUPEFY [STOO-PUH-FIY] VERB:
TO STUN OR OVERWHELM WITH AMAZEMENT.
I SURE HOPE THIS ISN'T A **SWEVEN.**

I'VE BEEN READING YOUR DAD'S DICTIONARY, SHE SAYS, SMILING.
WHERE'D YOU GET THAT?
MR. MAC SHOWED IT TO US AT BOOK CLUB. A LOT OF COOL WORDS.
WOW! THAT'S, UH, INTERESTING. I WOULDN'T SAY IT'S COOL, THOUGH.
WHAT LETTER ARE YOU ON?
X.

WOW, ALMOST FINISHED.
I'VE BEEN READING IT FOR, LIKE, THREE YEARS.

WHOA! TELL ME AN **X** WORD.
XU.

SOUNDS LIKE A **Z**.
YEAH. MOST OF THE X WORDS ARE PRONOUNCED LIKE THAT.

WHAT DOES IT MEAN?
IT'S THE MONEY THEY USED IN VIETNAM, BEFORE THE WAR.
LIKE A DOLLAR, ONLY A XU, SHE SAYS, AND YOU STARE AT HER LIPS
WAY TOO LONG.

EXACTLY.

WELL, I SEE MS. HARDWICK GAVE YOU THE **BROKEN PIECES** BOOK.
IT'S REALLY GOOD.

YOU READ IT?

YEP, AND, GET THIS: THE BOY IN THE BOOK IS REALLY GOOD AT
BASEBALL, AND HE'S FROM VIETNAM. YOU'LL LIKE IT, TRUST ME.
(DID SHE JUST SAY **GET THIS?**)

OKAY, WELL, GOTTA GO. TEXT ME, LET ME KNOW WHAT YOU
THINK OF THE BOOK.

UH, OKAY.

BYE, NICK. GET WELL SOON, 'CAUSE YOU AND I HAVE SOME DANCING
TO DO, AND SHE KISSES YOU GOODBYE ON THE FOREHEAD
MORE LIKE A GRANDMOTHER WOULD, BUT THAT'S NOT GOING TO
STOP YOU FROM NEVER WASHING YOUR HEAD.

EVER.

YOU'RE NOT REALLY INTO BASEBALL

BUT YOU GIVE THE BOOK A CHANCE FOR OBVIOUS REASONS, PLUS YOU NEED TO EARN SOME MINUTES.

ALL THE BROKEN PIECES

IS ABOUT WAR BUT TOLD BY A BOY YOUR AGE WHO CAN'T SEEM TO FIND PEACE AFTER A BOMB BLOWS HIS VILLAGE AND HIS BROTHER TO PIECES.

THEN A SOLDIER TAKES HIM TO AMERICA WHERE HE'S ADOPTED AND JUST ABOUT TO FIND OUT IF HE'S MADE THE BASEBALL TEAM ON PAGE **54** WHICH MEANS YOU HAVE AMASSED FOUR HOURS AND THIRTY MINUTES OF NONSTOP **TV.**

CLICK.

AFTER A NIGHT OF CHANNEL SURFING AND BACK-TO-BACK RERUNS OF **STAR TREK**, THE MORNING SUN RUSHES IN COURTESY OF THE NURSE RAISING THE BLINDS.

YOU EAT GOOEY FRUIT COCKTAIL AND JUST BEFORE YOU POWER UP YOUR TABLET, THE MAC STROLLS IN WITH HIS BOWLING BAG, AND DUFFEL, SPORTING A BLUE AND WHITE HOODIE THAT READS

PUT YOUR FACE IN A BOOK.

CONVERSATION WITH THE MAC

I BROUGHT YOU A GIFT, HE SAYS, HANDING YOU A BOX WRAPPED IN GIFT PAPER.

THE DRAGONFLY BOX?
WELL, IT IS A BOX, HE SAYS, PLOPPING HIMSELF DOWN IN THE CHAIR.

THANKS, MR. MAC, YOU SAY, OPENING THE GREASY, WHITE CARDBOARD BOX.

MR. MAC, THIS IS KFC!
YEP, SURE IS. BOUGHT YOU A THREE-PIECE CHICKEN MEAL AND A BISCUIT, HE SAYS.

UH, THANKS, BUT I CAN'T REALLY EAT THAT KIND OF STUFF YET, MR. MAC.
GOOD, 'CAUSE THERE'S ONLY ONE PIECE LEFT. GIVE IT HERE.
I DON'T KNOW IF I'M MORE HUNGRY OR TIRED, NICK.
. . .
I JUST WALKED FROM THE BOWLING ALLEY. IT WAS A TERRIBLE WALK, 'CAUSE I LOST.
WHY DIDN'T YOU DRIVE?
LUCKY FINALLY DIED. HAD IT FOR THIRTEEN YEARS.
GUESS YOUR LUCK RAN OUT, MR. MAC.
IF I WASN'T SO TIRED, I'D LAUGH AT THAT.
DID YOU GET THE BOOK?
YEP, I'M READING IT.
WHAT PAGE ARE YOU ON?
FIFTY-FOUR.
NICE!
ANY THOUGHTS?

YEAH, IT'S ALL POETRY.
AND?
IT'S OKAY.

SO WHY'RE YOU READING IT, IF IT'S JUST OKAY?
...
YOU'RE READING IT BECAUSE APRIL FARROW TOLD YOU TO
READ IT, HE SAYS, AND LAUGHS SO LOUD, THE PERSON IN THE
ROOM BEHIND YOU BANGS ON THE WALL.

SO WHAT DO YOU THINK OF THE MAIN
CHARACTER, MATT PIN?

I KINDA FEEL BAD FOR HIM, GETTING PICKED ON—
I CAN RELATE.

GETTING PICKED ON BY WHOM? THE MAC INTERRUPTS.

HIS CLASSMATES. THEY CALL HIM NAMES LIKE FROGFACE
AND MATT-THE-RAT AND RICE-PADDY AND—

ODD NAMES TO CALL SOMEONE,
DONTCHA THINK, NICK?

HE'S FROM VIETNAM,
SO THE KIDS TREAT
HIM DIFFERENT.

THEY'RE PREJUDICED,

I GUESS.

CAN'T WAIT TO FIND OUT WHAT HE DOES, 'CAUSE RIGHT NOW HE JUST DOES NOTHING.

WHAT WOULD YOU DO, NICK?

I'D PROBABLY STAND UP FOR MYSELF.

AND THEN THE MAC STOPS TALKING AND DRIFTS OFF, STARING OUT YOUR WINDOW AND YOU'RE LEFT WIDE AWAKE, THINKING OF ALL YOUR BROKEN PIECES.

READ ALOUD

WHEN HE WAKES UP TEN MINUTES LATER THE MAC WHIPS OUT HIS COPY, PLOPS DOWN IN THE VINYL CHAIR AT THE FOOT OF YOUR BED, KICKS OFF HIS WHITE HIGH-TOPS, PROPS BOTH LEGS UP, YAWNS LOUDER THAN AN ELEPHANT SEAL, STRETCHES, THEN PROCEEDS TO READ TO YOU LIKE YOU'RE IN KINDERGARTEN AND IT'S STORY TIME.

HE SOUNDS

LIKE HE'S ON THE MIKE, RAPPING.
HIS FLOW IS SICK.
HE POPS HIS SHOULDERS.
BOBS HIS HEAD.

ALL WHILE READING.
YOU LISTEN.
YOU LAUGH.

YOU FOLLOW ALONG.
DIDN'T THINK YOU WERE GONNA
LIKE THIS BOOK.

TWO HOURS LATER, WHEN THE MAC LANDS ON THE FINAL
PAGE, THE DOCTORS AND NURSES WHO'VE LINGERED
AND LISTENED, AND WHO CROWD YOUR ROOM,
GIVE THE MAC A STANDING OVATION.

TEXTS TO APRIL

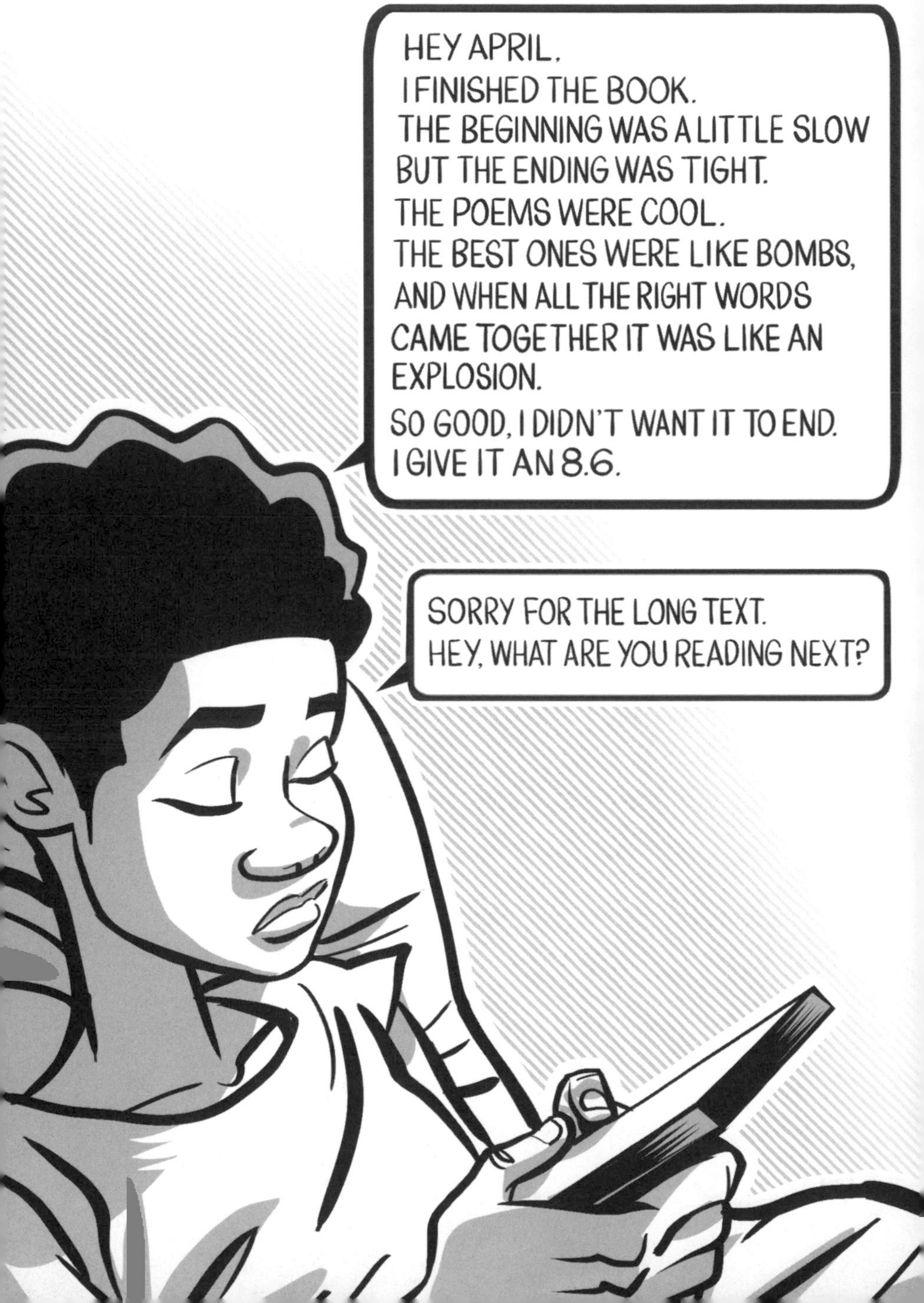

TEXTS FROM APRIL

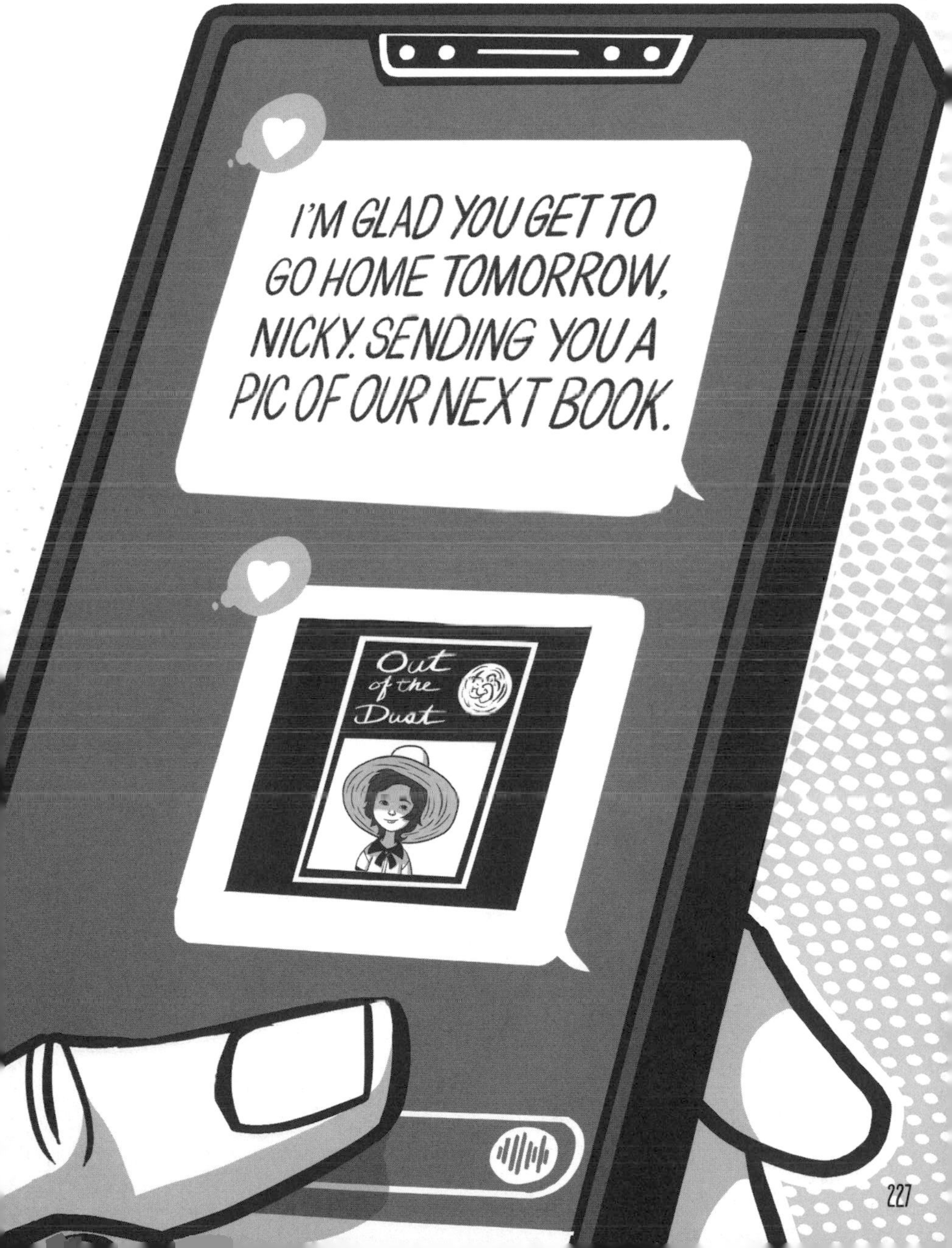

I'M GLAD YOU GET TO GO HOME TOMORROW, NICKY. SENDING YOU A PIC OF OUR NEXT BOOK.
Out of the Dust

DRIVING HOME

SHOTGUN, YOU YELL.

HOW MUCH TV DID YOU WATCH? MOM SAYS FROM THE
BACK SEAT.

A LOT. READ A BOOK, TOO.

REALLY?

YEP.

AND YOU LIKED IT?

UH, YEAH, YOU SAY. CAN WE STOP BY THE LIBRARY?
I NEED TO GET ANOTHER ONE.

SURE, AND AFTER LUNCH I CAN BEAT YOU IN PING-PONG,
MOM ANSWERS.

NAW. I MEAN NO, I'M GONNA JUST CHILL OUT IN MY ROOM.
I'M A LITTLE TIRED, YOU LIE.

OUT OF THE DUST

IS A STORY ABOUT A LANKY PIANO-PLAYING GIRL NAMED BILLIE JO WHOSE MOTHER IS GONE, WHOSE FATHER'S HEART AND SOUL ARE DISAPPEARING INTO THE DUST THAT BLANKETS THEIR OKLAHOMA TOWN,

AND EVEN THOUGH THE FIRST 59 PAGES RAIN DOWN HARD ON YOU, WHEN YOU GET TO PAGE 60 THE MONSOON COMES AND THE BOOK IS **UNPUTDOWNABLE.**

YOU DIAL APRIL'S NUMBER

SIX TIMES, BUT EACH TIME YOU HANG UP BEFORE IT RINGS BECAUSE YOU'RE NERVOUS AND DON'T KNOW WHAT TO SAY, SO BEFORE THE SEVENTH TIME YOU DECIDE TO WRITE DOWN A LIST OF EVERYTHING YOU WANT TO SAY TO HER, BUT YOU DON'T PLAN ON HER FATHER ANSWERING.

PHONE CONVERSATION

UH, HELLO, MR. FARROW, IS, UH, APRIL AVAILABLE?
WHO IS THIS CALLING?

IT'S ME, SIR, NICHOLAS, HER FRIEND FROM SCHOOL.
HER FRIEND FROM SCHOOL. I'VE NEVER MET YOU.

UH.
WELL, WHAT DO YOU WANT, SON?

I'D LIKE TO SPEAK TO HER, PLEASE, SIR.
ABOUT WHAT?

ABOUT, UH, A BOOK THAT
WE'RE READING.

DAD, GIVE ME THE PHONE. **STOP,** YOU HEAR APRIL SCREAM
IN THE BACKGROUND.

WELL, NICHOLAS, YOU HAVE TEN MINUTES
TO SPEAK TO MY DAUGHTER ABOUT THIS
BOOK THAT YOU'RE READING, YOU UNDERSTAND?

YES SIR.

HI, NICK, MY DAD CAN BE SO LAME SOME TIMES, SHE WHISPERS.

IT'S OKAY.

WHAT ARE YOU DOING?

I HAVE JUST COMPLETED OUT OF THE DUST, YOU ANSWER, READING FROM YOUR NOTES.

SWEET! WHAT DID YOU THINK?

IT WAS STELLAR, AND I WAS QUITE MOVED BY ITS CONTEMPLATION OF THE HUMAN SPIRIT.

WHY ARE YOU TALKING LIKE THAT, NICK?

LIKE WHAT?

YOU SOUND LIKE A ROBOT?

I AM VERY MUCH LOOKING FORWARD TO THE NEXT BOOK WE ARE READING.

STOP ACTING SILLY, NICK.

. . .

I WAS THINKING THAT YOU COULD PICK THE NEXT BOOK, NICK.

ME?

YEAH. THE BOOK CLUB NEEDS TO MIX IT UP A LITTLE.

BUT, UH, I'M NOT IN THE BOOK CLUB.

WELL, YOU KINDA ARE NOW, NICKY.
OKAY, YOU SAY, LAUGHING A LITTLE.

I'M SERIOUS, YOU'RE OFFICIAL NOW.
NO, IT'S NOT THAT. MY MOM CALLS ME NICKY.

OH, I'M SORRY.
NO, YOU CAN CALL ME THAT.

OKAY. HOW IS YOUR MOM DOING?
SHE'S FINE.

SHE'S STILL HERE?
YEAH, I THINK SHE'S GONNA STAY.

VERY COOL!

233

SO, YOU'RE GONNA PICK A BOOK.
YEAH, I GUESS.
MAYBE WE CAN DISCUSS THE BOOK AT YOUR HOUSE
OR SOMETHING.
UH, I DON'T KNOW ABOUT THAT. MY PARENTS PROBABLY
WON'T LET ME DO TH—
MAYBE YOU COULD ASK YOUR MOM, NICKY?

. . .

SO WHAT ARE YOU DOING NOW?
I AM PRESENTLY FOLDING MY CLOTHES AND
PREPARING TO CLEAN
UP MY ROOM.
OH, NICKY, YOU'RE
CRAY-CRAY.

. . .

BOOKS YOU FIND ON GOOGLE

DEAR KNOW IT ALL
PERCY JACKSON IF YOU'RE READING THIS,
IT'S **TOO LATE!**
PLANET MIDDLE SCHOOL
MAY B.
CATCHING FIRE!
BECAUSE. OF. **WINN-DIXIE.**
SMILE
I WILL SAVE YOU
WHEN YOU REACH ME
WHERE THE SIDEWALK
ENDS
UNTIL WE MEET AGAIN
PEACE,
LOCOMOTION
DARIUS AND TWIG
THE OUTSIDERS
P.S. BE ELEVEN

DREAMS COME TRUE

MS. HARDWICK'S MOVING TO ANOTHER
STATE TO TEACH

THE TWINS GOT KICKED
OUT FOR THE REST OF THE YEAR

APRIL'S COMING TO YOUR HOUSE
YOUR FAMILY IS BACK TOGETHER

AND YOU START
BACK SOCCER
SOON.

FINALLY, NORMAL SEEMS
POSSIBLE AGAIN.

TODAY, COBY CALLED

WHEN HE GOT BACK FROM DALLAS. ASKED YOU TO COME OVER.

YOU SAID NO, TOLD HIM YOU HAD TO CLEAN UP, WHICH WAS HALF TRUE.

YOU DIDN'T **HAVE** TO, YOU **WANTED TO**, 'CAUSE MOM SAID THE ONLY WAY SHE'D LET APRIL COME OVER WAS IF YOU CLEANED THE REFRIGERATOR, YOUR BATHROOM, AND YOUR ROOM, AND ORGANIZED THE CLOSET.

SO YOU LIMPED AROUND AND DID JUST THAT HAPPILY.

KNOCK KNOCK

YOUR MOTHER ANSWERS THE DOOR, AND YOU HEAR APRIL'S VOICE, BUT WAIT: SHE IS NOT ALONE.

ARGGGH!

TWAIN*

THANKS FOR INVITING US, NICK, APRIL SAYS. **US?** MOM SHOOTS YOU A LOOK LIKE YOU KNEW ALL THESE PEOPLE WERE COMING.

YOU DIDN'T!

SAIDA AND MAISHA ARE BEHIND APRIL, FOLLOWED BY ANNIE, KELLIE, AND, **GET THIS**, WINNIFRED.

*TWAIN [TWAYN] ADJECTIVE: TWO. THIS DANCE WAS SUPPOSED TO BE A TWO-STEP, NOT A FREAKIN' FLASH MOB.

NERDS AND WORDS

I CAN'T EVEN IMAGINE LIVING IN A DUST STORM, SAYS KELLIE.

I REALLY FELT LIKE I WAS RIGHT THERE WITH BILLIE JO.

YEAH, ME TOO, SAYS SAIDA, 'CAUSE MY DAD IS SAD A LOT TOO.

HE'S SAD BECAUSE HE LOST HIS JOB, MAISHA SAYS TO HER
SISTER, AND THEN WE'RE ALL QUIET, 'CAUSE THAT **IS** SAD.

WELL, I LIKE THAT MAD DOG LIKES HER,
BUT WHY DOESN'T HE JUST TELL HER? ANNIE SAYS.

YOU MEAN LIKE YOU WISH ROBBIE HOWARD WOULD TELL YOU?
KELLIE GIGGLES.

AND THAT'S WHEN YOU REALIZE YOU'RE IN A
BOOK CLUB WITH ALL GIRLS, WHICH IS INSANE.

APRIL SMILES AT YOU.

WHAT DO YOU THINK, NICK? SHE ASKS.

JUST THEN, YOUR MOM COMES OUT OF THE KITCHEN WITH A TRAY OF COOKIES, AND, **GET THIS**, TEA, AND NOW YOU'RE SIPPING TEA WITH A BUNCH OF GIRLS, AND SO GLAD THAT NO GUYS ARE HERE TO SEE YOU.

WHAT WERE YOU ABOUT TO SAY, NICK?

UH, I WAS JUST GONNA, UH, SAY THAT I LIKED IT, I GUESS.

DID YOU HAVE A FAVORITE PART? SHE ASKS.

YOU KNOW YOUR MOM'S LISTENING FROM THE KITCHEN WHEN YOU SAY, YEAH, **ON PAGE 205 WHEN BILLIE JO TELLS HER DAD, I CAN'T BE MY OWN MOTHER...**

A LONG WALK TO WATER

AT THE END OF THE MEETING WINNIFRED STARTS BLABBERING ABOUT SOME BOOK WE **MUST READ NEXT** BECAUSE HER OLDER SISTER SAYS IT'S HAUNTINGLY BEAUTIFUL AND GUT-WRENCHING AND IT'S BASED ON A TRUE STORY ABOUT BOY SOLDIERS IN SUDAN AND SHE GAVE IT FIVE STARS AND

BLAH BLAH BLAH

AND APRIL INTERRUPTS WITH:

I THINK NICKY HAS A **SUGGESTION.**

YOUR SUGGESTION

CAN WE PLEASE CHOOSE A BOOK WITH A BOY THIS TIME—

WEREN'T YOU LISTENING? WINEY INTERRUPTS. IT IS ABOUT A BOY.

PREFERABLY IN THIS TIME PERIOD, YOU CONTINUE.

I NEED A BREAK FROM HISTORY, I'M JUST SAYIN'.
LIKE WHAT? WINNIFRED WHINES.
LIKE PEACE, LOCOMOTION,
AN EPISTOLARY NOVEL, WHICH MEANS A—
I KNOW WHAT EPISTOLARY MEANS, SHE SHOUTS, STILL
FROWNING. IT'S A BOOK WRITTEN IN LETTERS.

GREAT CHOICE, APRIL SAYS, AND WINKS AT YOU.

BYE, NICK

THANKS FOR HOSTING THE CLUB, SHE SAYS,
AND HUGS YOU.

TELL YOUR MOM I CAN'T WAIT FOR TOMORROW.
HUH?

FAMILY MEETING

WHY'D YOU GO AND DO THAT?
I THOUGHT YOU'D LIKE IT, NICKY. IT'LL BE FUN.

WHAT IF I NEED MY CRUTCHES?
MY ANKLE'S STILL A LITTLE SORE.
YOU'LL BE ON A HORSE—WHY DO YOU NEED CRUTCHES?

MOM, IT'S NOT FAIR. YOU CAN'T JUST BE SETTING UP A
DATE FOR ME.
IT'S NOT A DATE. IT'S JUST ME, YOU, AND APRIL RIDING HORSES.

. . .

WELL, I LIKE HER. SHE'S A NICE GIRL.
YEAH, I KNOW.

I WAS THINKING THAT FOR THE
WEDDING, WE WOULD—

245

STOP MAKING FUN!

WHAT'S ALL THE COMMOTION? DAD SAYS, COMING IN THROUGH THE GARAGE.

WELL, YOUR EIGHTH GRADE SON IS AFRAID OF A GIRL.

I'M NOT AFRAID, DAD. SHE'S JUST SETTING UP OUTINGS AND WHATNOT WITHOUT MY PERMISSION.

I'M AFRAID THIS IS GROUNDS FOR A FAMILY MEETING. MEET ME IN THE LIVING ROOM.

WE'RE ALREADY IN THE LIVING ROOM, DAD.

RIGHT! OKAY. WELL, PRESENT YOUR CASE.

YOU START TALKING AND DAD INTERRUPTS —

LADIES FIRST, SIR.

THANK YOU, MOM SAYS, ALL PRIM AND PROPER-LIKE.
WELL, I MET HIS GIRLFRIEND—
SHE'S NOT MY GIRLFRIEND, I OBJECT.
SO NOTED, SAYS DAD. CARRY ON, MILADY.
I FIGURED HE MIGHT WANT TO HANG WITH
HER OUTSIDE OF SCHOOL, AND THOUGHT SINCE
HE'S SO GOOD AT RIDING—
NICHOLAS, ARE YOU GOOD AT RIDING?
DAD, THIS ISN'T ABOUT—
JUST ANSWER THE QUESTION, PLEASE.
YES.
DO YOU LIKE THIS APRIL GIRL?
UH, I GUESS.
YES OR NO ANSWER, PLEASE.
YEAH.

WILL YOU HAVE FUN WITH HER?

PROBABLY, BUT I'M NOT FULLY RECOVERED, AND—

ARE YOU GOING BACK TO SCHOOL NEXT WEEK?

YES.

BASED ON THE EVIDENCE THAT'S BEEN PRESENTED,
I RULE IN FAVOR OF THE DEFENDANT.

THE DATE SHALL COMMENCE TOMORROW.

WOOHOO! MOM YELLS.

THAT'S NOT FAIR, YOU SAY.

THE JUDGE HAS DECIDED, MOM COUNTERS.

LET'S HUG IT OUT, DAD SAYS, AND THE THREE OF YOU DO,
JUST LIKE OLD TIMES AND
HOPEFULLY NEW
ONES, TOO.

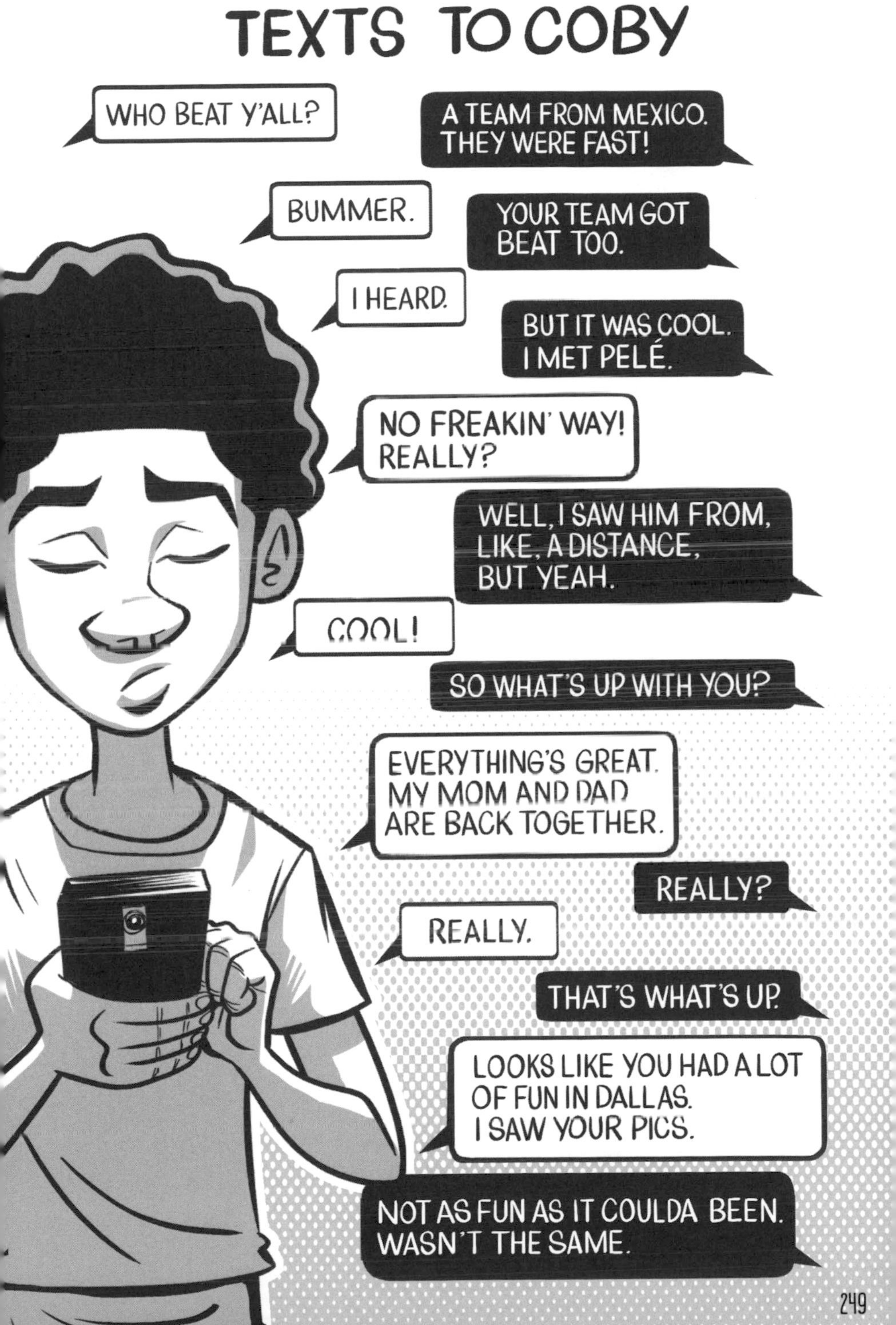
TEXTS TO COBY
WHO BEAT Y'ALL?
A TEAM FROM MEXICO. THEY WERE FAST!
BUMMER.
YOUR TEAM GOT BEAT TOO.
I HEARD.
BUT IT WAS COOL. I MET PELÉ.
NO FREAKIN' WAY! REALLY?
WELL, I SAW HIM FROM, LIKE, A DISTANCE, BUT YEAH.
COOL!
SO WHAT'S UP WITH YOU?
EVERYTHING'S GREAT. MY MOM AND DAD ARE BACK TOGETHER.
REALLY?
REALLY.
THAT'S WHAT'S UP.
LOOKS LIKE YOU HAD A LOT OF FUN IN DALLAS. I SAW YOUR PICS.
NOT AS FUN AS IT COULDA BEEN. WASN'T THE SAME.

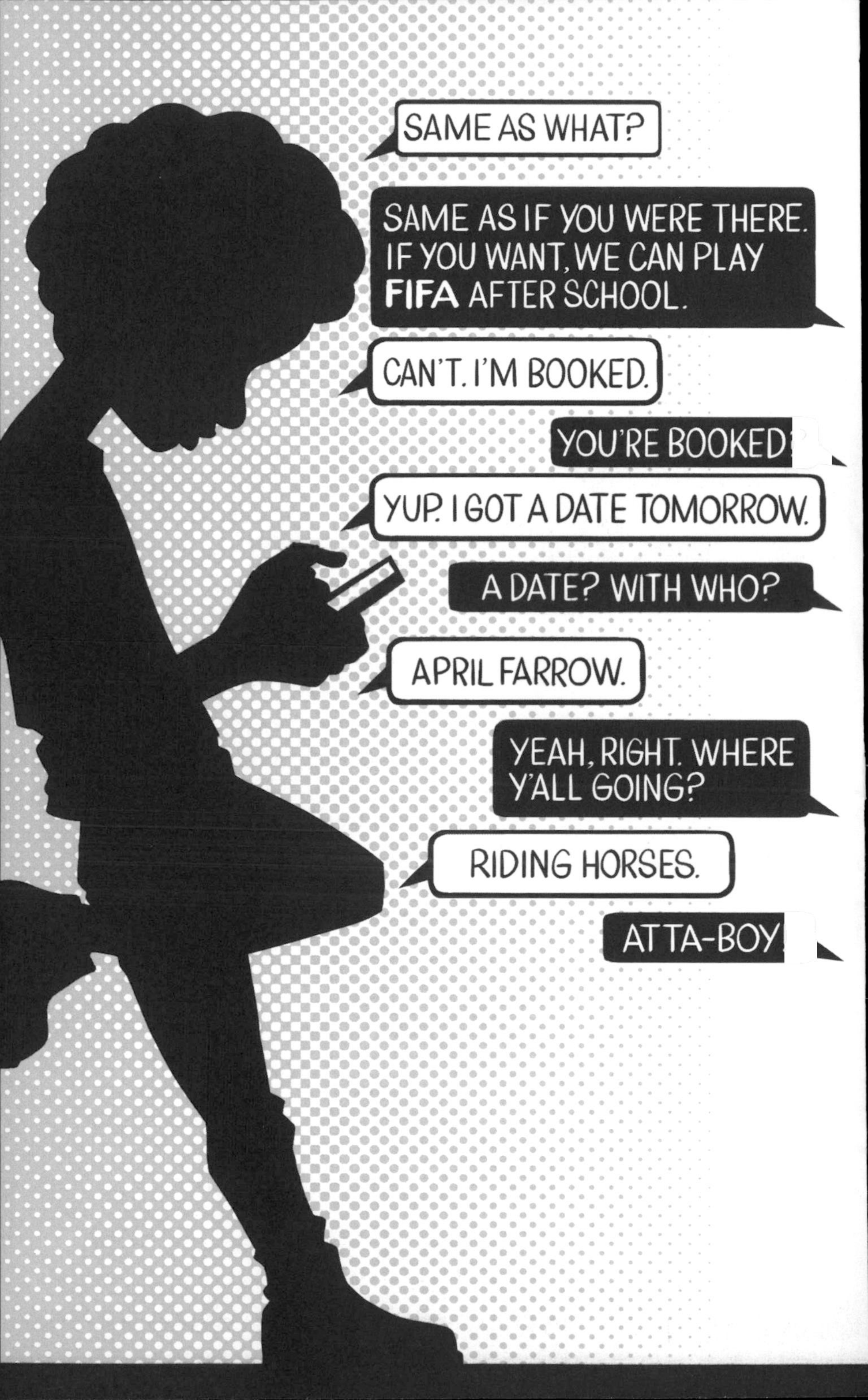
SAME AS WHAT?
SAME AS IF YOU WERE THERE. IF YOU WANT, WE CAN PLAY **FIFA** AFTER SCHOOL.
CAN'T. I'M BOOKED.
YOU'RE BOOKED
YUP. I GOT A DATE TOMORROW.
A DATE? WITH WHO?
APRIL FARROW.
YEAH, RIGHT. WHERE Y'ALL GOING?
RIDING HORSES.
ATTA-BOY

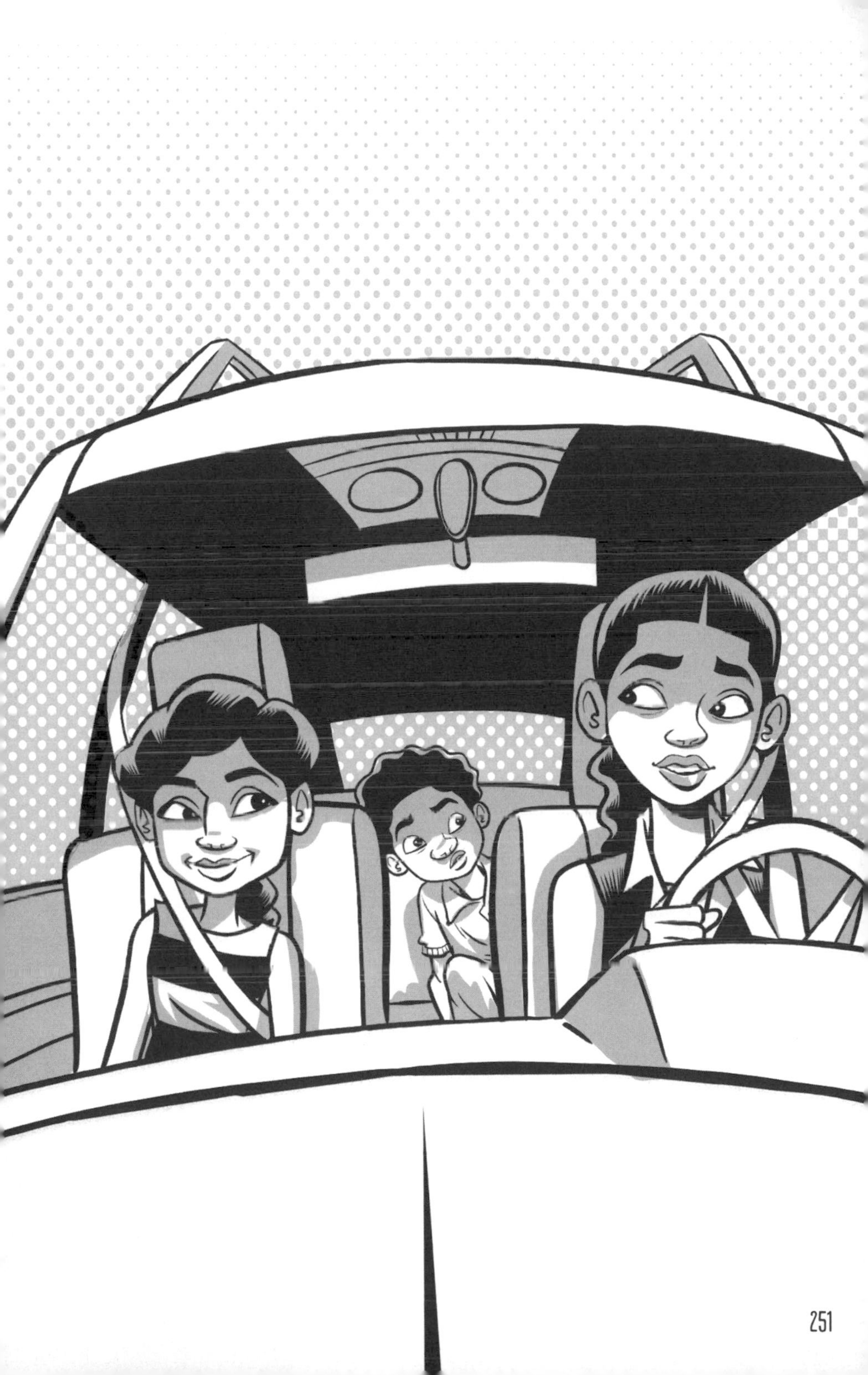

ROCK HORSE RANCH

USE THE STEEL COMB LIKE THIS, YOU SAY TO APRIL, DEMONSTRATING HOW TO REMOVE THE CAKED-ON DIRT.

THEN TAKE THIS SOFT BRUSH AND RUB OVER HER, YEP, JUST LIKE THAT, TO WASH AWAY THE DUST.

YOU'RE DOING GREAT, APRIL.

YOU KNOW A LOT ABOUT HORSES, NICK, SHE SAYS.
I GUESS.

YOU KNOW A LOT ABOUT EVERYTHING. IS IT TRUE YOU
SKIPPED A GRADE?
YEAH, SECOND.

YOU'RE SO SMART, NICKY.
. . .

OKAY, CHECK HER FEET WITH A HOOF PICK. TO CLEAR OUT
THE LITTLE ROCKS AND STUFF, YOU SAY.

ARE YOU FEELING BETTER, NICK?

YEAH, PRETTY MUCH.

ARE YOU STILL GONNA PLAY SOCCER?

UH, YEAH!

WELL, THAT'S GOOD. 'CAUSE YOU'RE PRETTY GOOD.

I KNOW.

(WE BOTH LAUGH.)

MISS QUATTLEBAUM TOLD ME TO TELL YOU HI.

MAYBE I'LL BE IN CLASS ON MONDAY, MILADY, YOU SAY,
NOT LOOKING UP, AND WISHING YOU HADN'T SAID THAT.
LET'S MOUNT THIS PONY, SHE SAYS.

WHOA, COWGIRL, YOU TELL HER. **WE STILL HAVE TO PUT THE SADDLE ON.**

OH, RIGHT. SORRY, NICK.

LET ME DO THE SADDLE, IT'S KIND OF HEAVY.
WANT ME TO HELP YOU, NICK?
I'M GOOD.
BUT YOU'RE NOT, 'CAUSE YOU STUMBLE, FALL FLAT ON YOUR
RUMPELSTILTSKIN.
HAVING TROUBLE OVER THERE? MOM HOLLERS, LAUGHING.
NOW APRIL'S TRYING NOT TO LAUGH. AND FAILING.
EVEN THE HORSE GOT JOKES. HE NEIGHS.
LET ME HELP YOU UP, COWBOY, APRIL SAYS, GRINNING.
YOU OKAY?
I'M GOOD.

255

YOU SAID THAT BEFORE, MOM HOLLERS. STILL LAUGHING.

YOU JUMP UP, SADDLE THE HORSE.

YEP, LET ME HELP YOU UP.

MOM COMES OVER WITH HER HORSE.

I'VE GOT AN IDEA, NICKY, SHE SAYS. IT'S HER FIRST TIME, SO ONE OF US NEEDS TO PULL APRIL'S HORSE AROUND UNTIL SHE GETS THE FEEL FOR IT.

I THOUGHT YOU WERE GOING TO DO IT, MOM?

UH, NO, MOMMA'S GONNA BE RIDING.

**WELL, I CAN'T DO IT.
I'M RIDING TOO.**

I'LL BE FINE, MRS. HALL, APRIL SAYS.

MOM SHOOTS YOU A LOOK.

HERE'S MY IDEA, SHE SAYS.

HOW ABOUT FOR THE FIRST FEW TIMES AROUND
THE FIELD, APRIL RIDES WITH YOU.

SOLVES ALL OUR PROBLEMS, RIGHT?

SOUNDS LIKE A PLAN TO ME, APRIL SAYS.

BLACK
JACK.

AFTERWARD

PLEASE, MOM! WE JUST WANT TO GO TO THE MALL.
IT'S NOT THAT LATE.
HER PARENTS SAID SHE COULD GO.
WE'RE JUST GONNA WALK AROUND,
MAYBE SEE A MOVIE.
HER FRIEND CHARLENE CAN MEET
US THERE TOO.
YOU CAN COME ALSO.

THANK YOU!

THANK YOU!

BY THE WAY, WOULD
YOU MIND SITTING A FEW ROWS
IN FRONT OF US, LIKE MAYBE,
UH, TWENTY-ONE?

YOU ABSOLUTELY LOVE

IT EACH TIME A ZOMBIE LUNGES AT A HUMAN AND CHOMPS ON FLESH BECAUSE IT MAKES APRIL GRAB THE LEGS NEXT TO HERS, ONE OF WHICH IS YOURS.

THANK YOU

I HAD A GREAT TIME WITH YOU AND YOUR MOM. YOUR PARENTS ROCK!

YOU'RE SO LUCKY.

GUESS I AM.

LATER, AT DINNER

MOM AND DAD STOP WHISPERING WHEN YOU GET
TO THE TABLE.
NICKY, I MADE YOUR FAVORITE SHE SAYS.
LOBSTER MAC-AND-CHEESE.
FIGURED YOU NEEDED A BREAK FROM THE MUSTARD.
WE BOTH KINDA LAUGH.
AND I EVEN MADE CUPCAKES.
RED VELVET, DAD ADDS.
BY **MADE**, YOUR FATHER MEANS HE
MADE HIS WAY TO THE CUPCAKERY
AND BOUGHT THEM.
WE ALL LAUGH, AND IT FEELS LIKE
LOVE IS BACK, LIKE HOME AGAIN,
JUST LIKE IT'S SUPPOSED TO FEEL.

CONVERSATION WITH MOM AND DAD

NICKY?

YEP, MOM?

I'M LEAVING ON THURSDAY.

WHAT DO YOU MEAN?

I'VE GOT TO GET BACK TO WORK, HONEY.

BUT YOU'RE COMING BACK, RIGHT?

TO VISIT.

HUH? I DON'T UNDERSTAND.

THE DERBY'S COMING UP. IT'S MY OBLIGATION TO GET BITE MY DUST PREPARED. YOU UNDERSTAND, RIGHT, NICKY? THEY NEED ME.

BUT I THOUGHT YOU QUIT, MOM.

QUIT? WHY WOULD I—

I MEAN, IT'S JUST THAT ME, YOU, AND DAD HAVE BEEN... I MEAN, THINGS ARE NORMAL AGAIN.

NICHOLAS, YOUR MOTHER AND I HAVE DECIDED TO GET A DIVORCE.

A DIVORCE? BUT, I THOUGHT, UH, I JUST... I, WE—
I WAS AFRAID OF THIS, DAD SAYS TO MOM.

AFRAID OF WHAT, THAT I WOULD THINK YOU TWO WOULD GET YOUR LIFE TOGETHER AND NOT RUIN MINE AGAIN?
YOUR FATHER AND I LOVE EACH OTHER, AND WE ALWAYS WILL, BUT SOMETIMES LIFE AND WORK AND LOVE DON'T ALL MESH.

I DON'T EVEN KNOW WHAT THAT MEANS.
NICHOLAS, YOUR MOTHER AND I ARE JUST, UH, UNCOMPOSSIBLE.

IT'S IN, INCOMPOSSIBLE,* NOT UN. LOOK IT UP, YOU SAY,
AND START GETTING UP FROM THE TABLE.
WE'RE SORRY, HONEY.

YEAH, ME TOO. SORRY SOME HORSE'S NEEDS ARE MORE IMPORTANT THAN MINE.
NICKY, COME BACK. LET'S TALK ABOUT THIS.

. . .

* INCOMPOSSIBLE [IN-KUHM-POS-UH-BUHL]
ADJECTIVE: INCAPABLE OF COEXISTING,
OF BEING TOGETHER.

IT'S OFFICIAL: EIGHTH GRADE SUCKS!

263

WHAT HAPPENS TO A DREAM DESTROYED?
DOES IT SINK
LIKE A WRECKED SHIP
IN THE SEA?
OR WADE IN THE WATER LIKE A BOY OVERBOARD?
MAYBE IT JUST FLOATS
AROUND AND AROUND...
OR DOES IT DROWN?

ON THE WAY TO THE AIRPORT

MOM TELLS YOU HOW PROUD SHE IS OF THE MAN YOU'RE BECOMING AND MAKES YOU PROMISE TO CALL OR TEXT HER EVERY DAY, EAT HEALTHIER, QUIT CUTTING YOUR NAILS ON THE LIVING ROOM FLOOR, AND KEEP YOUR GRADES UP.

MAYBE YOU AND COBY WANT TO COME TO THE DERBY, SHE ADDS.

NO THANKS, WE HAVE SOCCER OBLIGATIONS, YOU ANSWER.

265

SINKING

IN THE CAR ON THE WAY HOME THE ENGINE BATTLES THE HUM OF SILENCE AND SADNESS THAT ENVELOPS YOU.

HE FINALLY SAYS SOMETHING...RANDOM.

NICHOLAS, THE WORLD IS AN INFINITE SEA OF ENDLESS POSSIBILITY.

YEAH, WELL, IT FEELS LIKE THERE'S A BIG FREAKIN' HOLE IN MY SHIP, DAD.

CONVERSATION WITH DR. FRAUD

IS EMINEM YOUR FAVORITE RAPPER?
HUH?

THE LAST TIME WE SPOKE, YOU WERE QUOTING HIM.
HE'S NOT MY FAVORITE RAPPER, THOUGH.

HOW DID YOU DECIDE TO HANDLE THE BULLYING?
IT'S HANDLED.

SO IT'S NOT AN ISSUE?
I DON'T THINK SO.

AND WHAT ABOUT YOUR BIKE?
UH, WHAT ABOUT IT?

DO YOU WANT IT BACK?
THOSE HELLKITES* ARE GONE, SO THAT'S ALL I REALLY WANTED.

* HELLKITE [HEL-KIYT] NOUN:
AN EXTREMELY CRUEL PERSON.
COBY SAYS THEY POSTED A
PIC OF MY BIKE AND A
BUNCH OF OTHER STUFF
THEY TOOK FROM KIDS.

NICE WORD. YOUR MOTHER MENTIONED YOU WERE EXCEPTIONALLY ARTICULATE.

DIDN'T REALLY HAVE A CHOICE ABOUT THAT.

WHAT DO YOU MEAN?

MY FATHER FORCES ME TO READ HIS DICTIONARY. HAS SINCE I WAS NINE.

WOULD YOU RATHER NOT BE EXCEPTIONALLY ARTICULATE?

MAYBE.

SO YOU'D JUST PREFER TO BE NORMAL?

I GUESS.

LIKE EVERYONE ELSE?

YEP.

EVEN ON THE SOCCER FIELD?

THAT'S DIFFERENT.

HOW?

I LIKE SOCCER.

AND YOU DON'T LIKE BEING SMART?

SIGMUND FREUD

I DON'T LIKE BEING FORCED TO **SOUND** SMART.

. . .

. . .

TELL ME, HOW DO YOU FEEL ABOUT YOUR MOTHER LEAVING?
I FEEL LIKE I'M DROWNING.

WHAT WILL IT TAKE FOR YOU TO GET ABOVE WATER?
I DON'T KNOW. IT'S OUTTA MY CONTROL. SHE'S NOT
COMING BACK AND THEY'RE GETTING DIVORCED.

CAN YOU SWIM?
UH, YEAH!

SO IF YOU FEEL LIKE YOU'RE DROWNING AND YOU KNOW
HOW TO SWIM, THEN MAYBE YOU CAN GET ABOVE WATER.

THAT SOUNDS CRAZY.

I GUESS IT DOES.

. . .

HOW ARE THINGS GOING
IN SCHOOL?
SCHOOL'S OKAY, BUT
I'M TIRED A LOT.

ARE YOU GETTING SLEEP
AT NIGHT?
I WAS.
PROBABLY NOT NOW.

WHY NOT?
'CAUSE I'LL BE THINKING ABOUT MY MOM.

HOW LONG HAS SHE BEEN GONE?
THREE DAYS, THIS TIME.

HAVE YOU SPOKEN TO HER?
WHEN SHE GOT TO HER, UH, NEW HOUSE SHE CALLED.

AND SINCE THEN?
NOPE.

MAYBE YOU SHOULD CALL OR TEXT HER.
YEAH!

AS HARD AS IT IS, REGULAR COMMUNICATION IS WHAT GETS THINGS BACK TO NORMAL.

NORMAL? YEAH, RIGHT.

CHANGE IS HARD. NICHOLAS FOR ALL OF US. WE FIGURE OUT HOW TO COPE.

HOW TO ADAPT, AND EVENTUALLY THINGS DO GET BACK TO NORMAL.

YEAH!

. . .

. . .

TALKING ABOUT THINGS IS GOOD. IT CAN HELP YOU STAY ABOVE WATER.
OH, REALLY?
YES.
...
SO, I'LL SEE YOU NEXT WEEK?
TUPAC.
I'M SORRY?
YOU ASKED WHO MY FAVORITE RAPPER WAS. IT'S TUPAC.
KEEP YOUR HEAD UP, NICHOLAS.
YEAH.

REGULAR COMMUNICATION

HEY, MOM, I'M GOOD, THOUGH MY TOENAILS HAVE GROWN SO LONG THAT MY HOOVES HURT BAD.

APRIL SAYS HI.

AT MISS QUATTLEBAUM'S

THE GIRLS LINE UP EAR TO EAR SO YOU AND THE OTHER
BOYS CAN GREET THEM WITH A PROPER HAND KISS.

GENTLEMEN, BACKS ARE STRAIGHT AND STIFF,
MISS FRUIT TREE SAYS.

SHE PASSES OUT GLOVES TO THE GIRLS,
SO THEY DON'T HAVE TO TOUCH OUR
CLAMMY HANDS, YOU GUESS.

HOLDING APRIL'S HAND, YOU DECIDE TO FINALLY WEAR COOL:

UH, APRIL, I WAS WONDERING, IF YOU, UH, WANTED TO GO TO THE EIGHTH GRADE FORMAL WITH ME?

REGULAR COMMUNICATION

HEY, MOM, I'M GOOD, THOUGH I'M A LITTLE SICK OF CHEETOS AND GRAPE SODA.

APRIL SAYS HI.

AFTER SCHOOL, YOU STOP IN TO SEE THE MAC

HEY, NICK, DID YOU KNOW THAT OUTSIDE OF A DOG, A BOOK IS A MAN'S BEST FRIEND, AND INSIDE OF A DOG, IT'S TOO DARK TO READ? HE SAYS, LAUGHING.

C'MON, YOU KNOW THAT WAS FUNNY.

IT WAS CORNY, MR. MAC.

BEFORE YOU LEAVE, GRAB YOUR FLASH DRIVE OUT OF LOST AND FOUND.

OH, SNAP! BEEN LOOKING FOR THAT.

IT'S GOT MY OUTLINE ON IT.

YOU LEFT IT IN THE COMPUTER.

DANG, I SURE DID.

SO, NO SOCCER PRACTICE TODAY? WHAT'S UP?

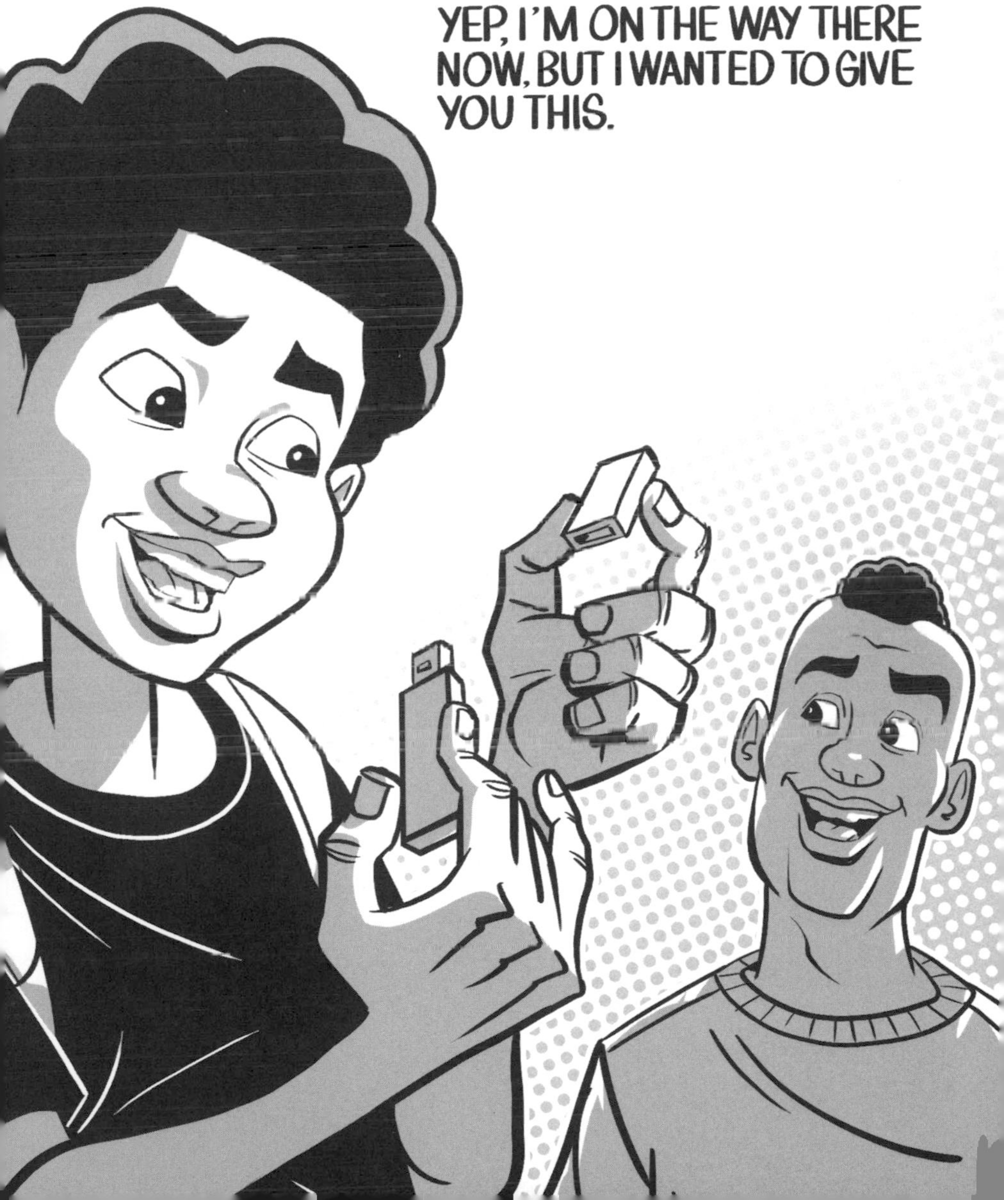
YEP, I'M ON THE WAY THERE NOW, BUT I WANTED TO GIVE YOU THIS.

WHAT'S THIS?

A BIRTHDAY GIFT.

FOR ME? HOW'D YOU KNOW IT WAS MY BIRTHDAY?

GOOGLE.

YOU STALKING ME, NICK HALL!

YOU WERE A PRETTY GOOD RAPPER, MR. MAC.

PRETTY GOOD? I WAS DOPE.

YOU'RE A COOL LIBRARIAN. THERE'S A SURPRISE IN THE BOOK.

OH SNAP, YOU DID ANOTHER BLACK OUT JOINT!

YEAH! PLUS, I READ THE WHOLE FREAKIN' BOOK.

HOW WAS IT?

IT WAS SAD, AND CRAZY FUNNY,
AND REALLY GOOD, AND I THINK YOU'LL
REALLY LIKE IT.

KID, YOU'RE THE REAL DEAL.
THIS MEANS A LOT.

HOW MUCH?
A WHOLE LOT.
SO MUCH THAT YOU'LL TELL ME WHAT'S INSIDE YOUR DRAGONFLY BOX?
YOU WANT A LOOK INSIDE FREEDOM?
HUH?
MY DRAGONFLY BOX. I CALL IT FREEDOM.
YOU NAME EVERYTHING, YOUR CAR, YOUR BOX—
WANNA KNOW WHAT I CALL MY BOWLING BALL?
UH, NO THANKS.
FINE, GO AHEAD, OPEN THE BOX.
SERIOUSLY?
GO FOR IT.
COOL!

WAIT, IT'S LOCKED.
WHERE'S THE KEY, MR. MAC?
YA GOTTA HAVE THE KEY
YA GOTTA HAVE THE KEY
YA GOTTA HAVE THE KEY
IF YA WANNA BE FREE.
THE MAC REPEATS THIS A
FEW TIMES, THEN TAKES
THE BOX BACK.

REAL FUNNY! HEY, MR. MAC, WHY ARE
YOU SO INTO DRAGONFLIES?
BECAUSE THEY'RE ELECTRIC, NICK.
LIKE BOLTS OF LIGHTNING, THEY
ROCKET INTO THE DAY.
THAT'S HOW I WANNA LIVE. YOU?

YEAH, UH, I GUESS.
WELL THEN, CARRY ON.
I'VE GOT SOME WORK TO FINISH.
YOU'VE GOT A CLERK TO DIMINISH?
YOU KNOW A JERK THAT'S FINNISH?
YOU'RE OFFICIALLY THE MALAPROP KING, NICK, HE SAYS.
THANKS AGAIN FOR THE BOOK.
NO PROBLEMO.

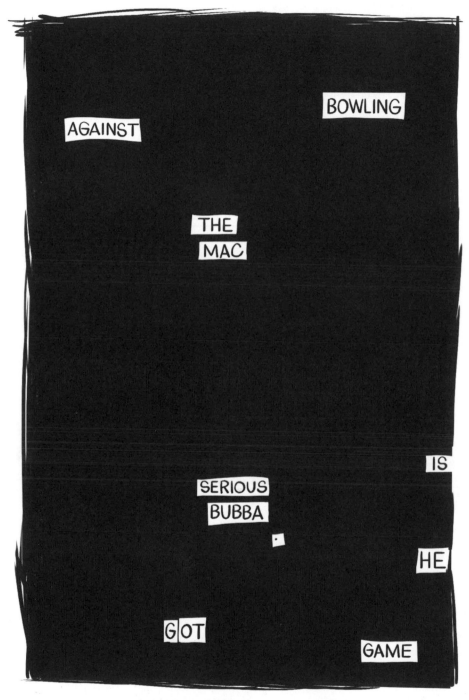

HOW LAMAR'S BAD PRANK WON A BUBBA-SIZED TROPHY

PLAYOFFS

APRIL COMES OVER TO WISH YOU LUCK BEFORE YOUR FIRST GAME BACK.

SCORE ONE FOR ME, SHE SAYS.

YOU DON'T.
YOU SCORE **TWO**.

TEXTS FROM MOM

NICKY, DIDN'T HEAR FROM YOU THIS WEEKEND.

HOW WAS THE GAME?

YOUR TEXTS ARE FUNNY. MISS YA!

REGULAR COMMUNICATION

HEY, MOM, I'M GOOD.
CAN'T TALK, AS I'M IN SCHOOL,
FAILING GRAVELY.
WHO CARES ABOUT GRADES?

WE WON!

WINNIFRED MAY BE A GADFLY*

BUT HER SLIDESHOW TRIBUTE TO MS. HARDWICK IS PRETTY SWELL AND IT SENDS US ALL TO SOB TOWN.

*GADFLY [GAD-FLY] NOUN: AN ANNOYING PERSON. IN THE DICTIONARY, THERE'S A PIC OF WINNIFRED NEXT TO THIS WORD.

WAITING AT THE BUS STOP WHEN A POLICE CAR PULLS UP

HEY, NICK, WE CAN TAKE YOU HOME.
NO THANKS, WE'RE GOOD, APRIL.
GET IN HERE, FELLAS, LOOKS LIKE IT'S ABOUT TO RAIN.
UH, OKAY, COBY SAYS, CLIMBING INTO THE BACK SEAT.
DAD, THIS IS NICK, REMEMBER?
OH, YEAH, I REMEMBER, FROM THE PHONE, RIGHT?
HE SHOOTS YOU A LOOK THROUGH THE REARVIEW MIRROR.
AND THIS IS HIS BEST FRIEND, COBY.
COOL RIDE, MR. FARROW.
DON'T GET USED TO IT, SON.
NO SIR.

I UNDERSTAND YOU PLAY SOCCER?
YES SIR, WE DO, YOU SAY.
WHO'S BETTER?
I AM, SIR, COBY SAYS, ALL POLITE.
NICHOLAS, HOW IS SCHOOL?
IT'S FINE, SIR.
Y'ALL STOP CALLING ME SIR. OFFICER IS FINE!
DAAAADDDDD, STOP!
APRIL TELLS ME YOU'RE A WORDSMITH
OR SOMETHING. YOU A WORDSMITH, NICHOLAS?
UH, I GUESS… OFFICER.

ARE YOU OR AREN'T YOU, SON?

DAAAADDDDD, WHY ARE YOU INTERROGATING HIM? LEAVE HIM ALONE.

I KNOW A LOT OF WORDS, IF THAT'S WHAT YOU'RE ASKING.
HE SURE DOES, APRIL BRAGS. NICK, TELL HIM ABOUT THAT WORD LIMERENCE.
YEAH, NICHOLAS, TELL ME ABOUT THAT WORD LIMERENCE, THE ONE THAT MY DAUGHTER HAS WRITTEN ON EVERY NOTEBOOK, PLASTERED ALL OVER HER DOOR, AND WHICH SHE NOW WANTS TO TATTOO ON THE BACK OF HER NECK. TELL. ME. ABOUT. THAT. WORD.
DAAAADDDDD, **STOP IT!**
THIS IS SO COOL, OFFICER, COBY BLURTS OUT.
UH, WHY IS THE SIREN ON?

THIRTY MINUTES LATER

MY DAD'S JUST TRYING TO SCARE YOU.
WELL, IT WORKED.
YOU COMING TO CHARLENE'S POOL PARTY?
I DON'T KNOW.
WELL, I THINK YOU SHOULD.
OKAY, MAYBE.
TRY AGAIN, NICKY.
YEAH, I GUESS.
BETTER. TEXT ME LATER.
OKAY. THANKS FOR THE RIDE.
I CAN'T KISS YOU ON THE CHEEK, 'CAUSE MY DAD IS LOOK—

GOODBYE, NICHOLAS, HER DAD
SCREAMS FROM THE CAR, THEN TURNS ON
THE SIREN. AGAIN.

GEESH, I GOTTA GO, NICKY.

UH, UH. . . .
BYE. THANKS.

I'VE BEEN THINKING

MAYBE YOU TAKE A BREAK FROM MY DICTIONARY, SON.
THE IRONY OF THIS IS COLOSSAL.
YOU LAUGH LONG AND LOUD LIKE A GUINEA BABOON
BEING TICKLED. AND SO DOES HE WHEN YOU SAY:
**WELL THAT'S JUST PERFECT, DAD, 'CAUSE I FINISHED
IT LAST NIGHT.**

REALLY? WELL, THAT'S GREAT.
WE SHOULD CELEBRATE.
YOU HUNGRY?

VERY.
I'LL MAKE DINNER.

**HOW ABOUT NO, DAD.
LET'S GO OUT.**

GREAT. I GOT THE PERFECT PLACE.
NO WHITE TABLECLOTHS, DAD.

I WAS THINKING A SPORTS RESTAURANT.
UNLIMITED HOT WINGS AND SOCCER.

YEAH!

CONVERSATION WITH DAD

YOUR DAD IS ALWAYS FULL OF WORDS TO HURL AT YOU, BUT TONIGHT, FOR ONCE, HE'S WORDBOUND.* SO ARE YOU.

. . .

. . .

THESE WINGS ARE GOOD.
YEAH.

. . .

. . .

DAD, CAN I ASK YOU A QUESTION?
OF COURSE.

DID YOU EVER GET INTO A FIGHT AT SCHOOL?

*WORDBOUND [WURD-BOUND] ADJECTIVE: UNABLE TO FIND EXPRESSION IN WORDS. KINDA IRONIC, RIGHT?

FIGHTS? NO.

...

NOT AT...SCHOOL.

...

THERE WAS THIS KID AT CHURCH NAMED SKINNY
WHO PICKED ON ME.

REALLY?

HE SAT BEHIND ME IN SUNDAY SCHOOL AND WOULD
SLAP ME AND SPIT WATER ON ME. ONE TIME HE EVEN
TRIPPED ME AND I BUSTED MY LIP.
IT WAS EASTER AND I WAS WEARING A BRAND-NEW
WHITE SUIT.

OH, SNAP! WHAT DID YOU DO?

I RAN TO MY MOM,
BLEEDING AND CRYING.

OH.

BUT MY DAD CAME OVER
AND DRAGGED ME TO
THE BATHROOM.

**WHAT'D HE DO, FUSS
AT YOU?**

NO, HE CLEANED ME UP,
AND ASKED ME A QUESTION.

WHAT?

"WHAT WOULD YOU DO IF
YOU WEREN'T AFRAID?"

THAT'S WHAT HE ASKED YOU?

YEP, AND I TOLD HIM, MAYBE FIGHT HIM.

WHAT'D HE SAY?

"BULLIES DON'T LIKE TO FIGHT, SON. THEY LIKE TO WIN. BEING AFRAID IS NORMAL. THE ONLY FIGHT YOU REALLY HAVE TO WIN IS THE ONE AGAINST THE FEAR."

WHAT DOES THAT EVEN MEAN?

AND THEN HE SAID, "YOU GOT THIS," AND WALKED OUT.

WHAT'D YOU DO?

I CRIED SOME MORE, THEN WENT BACK OUTSIDE, WHERE ALL THE KIDS WERE, AND WALKED RIGHT UP TO SKINNY, AND SAID, "SKINNY, I'M SICK OF YOUR YOBBERY."* AND THEN I PUT UP MY DUKES.

YOU, UH, PUT UP YOUR DUKES, DAD?

YEAH, I WAS READY TO FIGHT, NICK! I DODGED AND WEAVED LIKE MUHAMMAD ALI. HE LOOKED A LITTLE CONFUSED, MAYBE A LITTLE AFRAID. I CHARGED HIM LIKE A BULL, KNOCKED HIM TO THE GROUND.

THAT'S SO COOL, DAD. WHAT HAPPENED NEXT?

HE GOT UP AND PUNCHED ME IN THE EYE. I HAD A BLACK EYE FOR TWO WEEKS.

*YOBBERY [YOB-UH-REE] NOUN: HOOLIGANISM.

DANG! SORRY, DAD.
DON'T BE. YOUR GRANDDAD WAS RIGHT. SKINNY
STOPPED MESSING WITH ME AFTER THAT. I MEAN, HE
USED TO MAKE JOKES ABOUT ME, BUT EVEN THAT
STOPPED AFTER A WHILE.

THAT REALLY HAPPEN, DAD?
SURE DID.

SHOULD WE GET SOME MORE WINGS, DAD?
SHOULD WE KNIT SOME FLOOR SWINGS?

IT'S GOTTA MAKE SENSE, DAD.
SHOULD WE QUIT BEFORE SPRING?

WELL DONE, DAD.
GOOD, NOW LET'S ORDER
MORE WINGS.

HEY, MOM

DAD'S AT A CONFERENCE.
I'M HOME ALONE.
IT'S HOUSE PARTY TIME!

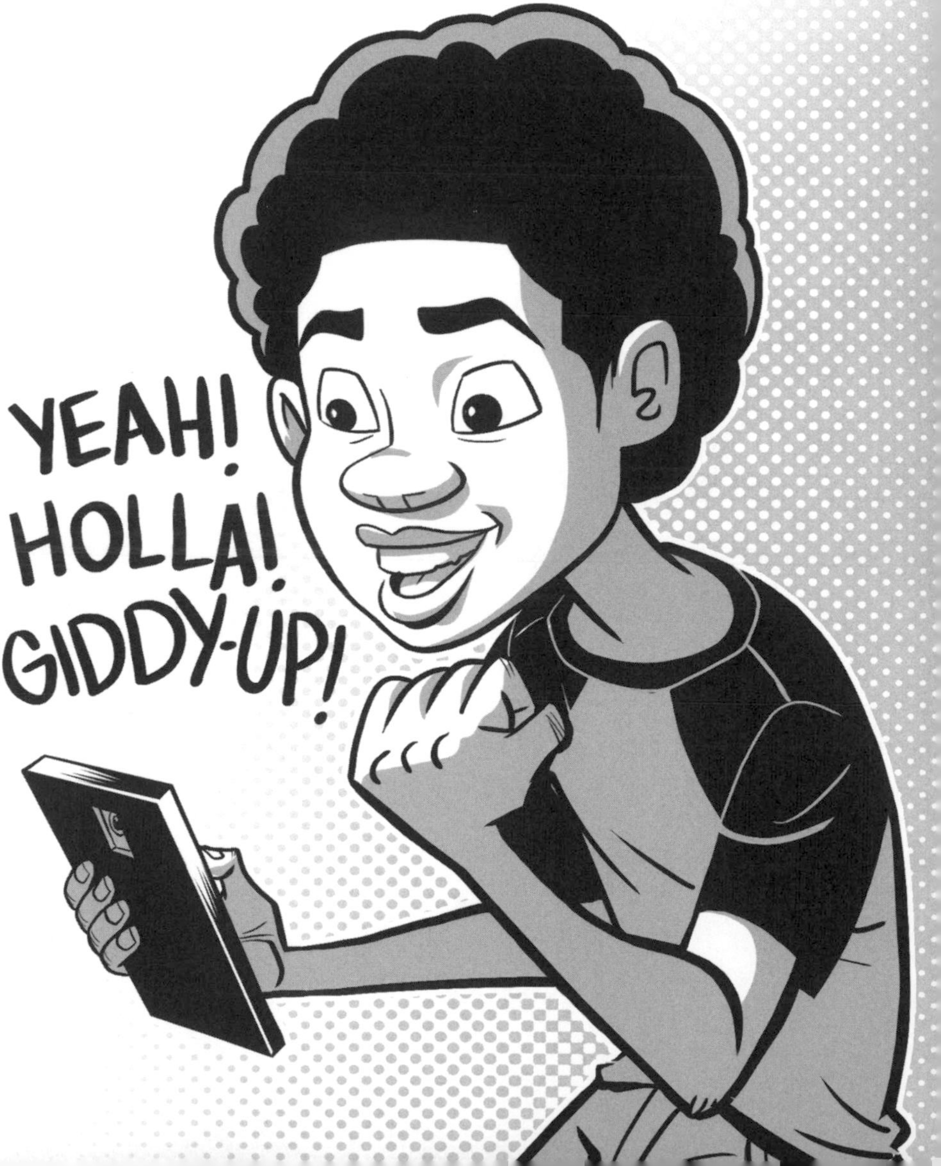

YEAH!
HOLLA!
GIDDY-UP!

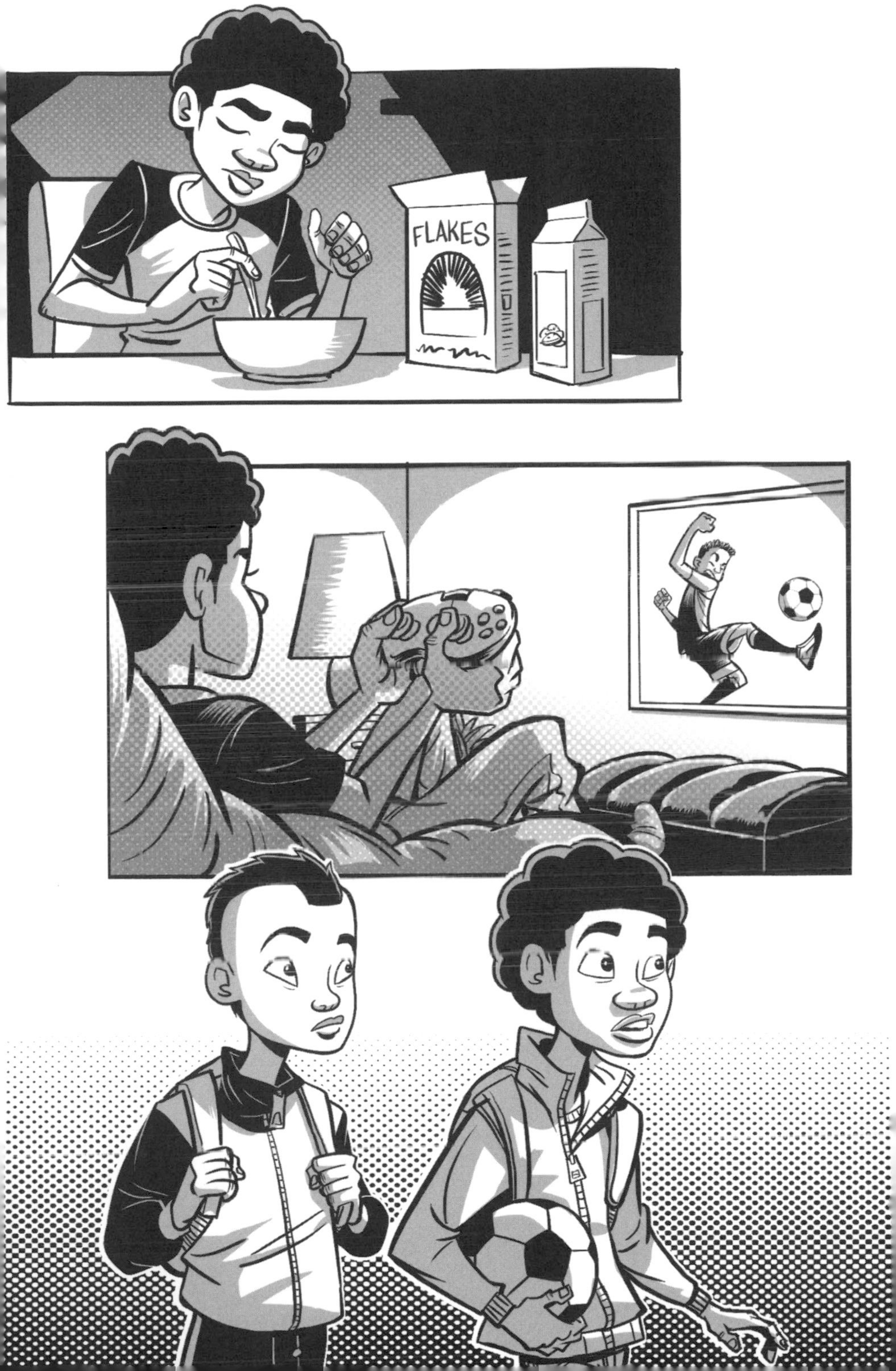
FLAKES

BLUE MOON RIVER

STANDING OUTSIDE LEANING AGAINST A LIGHT BLUE CONVERTIBLE CAR IS THE MAC.

HEY, MR. MAC. WHAT'S UP?

YOU FORGOT THIS. AGAIN, HE SAYS, HANDING YOU YOUR FLASH DRIVE.

THANKS. YOU ROCK, MR. MAC!

THAT'S YOUR NEW CAR?

BLUE MOON RIVER.

HUH?

IT'S A 1972 FORD MERCURY BROUGHAM MONTEGO DROP-TOP.

PRETTY ZAZZY!* INTERESTING NAME FOR A CAR, THOUGH.

*ZAZZY [ZAZ-EE] ADJECTIVE: STYLISH OR FLASHY.

NICHOLAS, THERE'S ONLY A HUNDRED OR SO OF THESE LEFT.

OH, I GET IT—IT'S RARE, LIKE ONCE IN A **BLUE MOON.**

EXACTLY! ME AND BLUE MOON RIVER ARE SEARCHING FOR THE RAINBOW'S END.

UH…OKAY, BUT WHY RIVER?

NICK, THE RIVER IS ALWAYS TURNING AND BENDING. YOU NEVER KNOW WHERE IT'S GOING TO GO AND WHERE YOU'LL WIND UP. FOLLOW THE BEND.

THAT'S PRETTY DEEP, MR. MAC.

STAY ON YOUR OWN PATH. DON'T LET ANYONE DETER YOU. EARTHA KITT SAID THAT.

WHO'S BERTHA SCHMIDT?

NICHOLAS, TURNS OUT MS. HARDWICK ISN'T THE ONLY ONE LEAVING, HE SAYS.

WHAT DO YOU MEAN?

LANGSTON HUGHES WILL BE LOOKING FOR A NEW LIBRARIAN, TOO.

YOU'RE NOT COMING BACK?

I'M NOT COMING BACK.

WHY?

BECAUSE THE RIVER TURNS, AND THERE'S A LOT OF WORLD TO SEE.

ARE YOU FOLLOWING MS. HARDWICK?

YOU'RE A SMART KID.

A NEW BOOK FOR YOU, HE SAYS, REACHING INTO THE BAG ON THE GROUND NEXT TO HIM.

THANKS. RHYME SCHEMER'S A DOPE TITLE, MR. MAC.
IS THIS YOUR AUTOBIOGRAPHY?
IT'S NOT, BUT YOU'RE GONNA DIG IT.
THE QUESTION IS, WILL IT RIP MY HEART OUT AND
STOMP ON IT?
I'M OUTTA HERE, HE SAYS, JUMPING INTO
BLUE MOON RIVER.
DON'T FORGET YOUR BAG, YOU SAY, PICKING IT UP TO
HAND TO HIM, BUT RIGHT BEFORE HE SPEEDS OFF
THE MAC YELLS, THAT'S YOURS TOO. BE COOL, NICK.

INSIDE THE BAG IS, GET THIS, FREEDOM

YOU UNLOCK THE MAC'S DRAGONFLY BOX FULLY
EXPECTING BURSTS OF ELECTRICITY TO FLITTER AND
FLUTTER LIKE BLUE LIGHTNING, LIKE SOULS ON FIRE.
WHAT YOU SEE IS EVEN BETTER.

SUB

COACH FINALLY PUTS YOU IN.
IT FEELS GOOD TO RUN TOWARD SOMETHING,
AND NOT AWAY. . .

AFTER THE GAME

AT CHARLENE'S POOL PARTY YOU SEE COBY, APRIL IN A PINK SWIMSUIT, AND, UH, YOUR BIKE.

YOU NOTICE THE TWINS

THERE'S A FIRST TIME FOR EVERYTHING, YOU THINK, AND A BLACK EYE OR A BRUISED RIB CAN'T HURT ANY MORE THAN **APPENDICITIS**.

I'LL BE RIGHT BACK, YOU TELL COBY.

HEY, DEAN, YOU SCREAM

HE TURNS AROUND.

ACTUALLY, EVERYONE AT THE PARTY TURNS AROUND.

I'M SICK OF YOUR YOBBERY.

YOU WANT SOME OF THIS?

APPARENTLY HE DOES, 'CAUSE HE COMES CHARGING AT YOU LIKE A RED BULL.

AS HE NEARS, YOU START, **GET THIS,** DODGING AND WEAVING AND SINGING IN YOUR BEST QUATTLEBAUM VOICE

ONE-TWO-THREE, TWO-TWO-THREE.

WHEN HE GETS TO YOU, YOU SLIDE SWIFTLY TO THE RIGHT, LIKE YOU'VE GOT THE BALL AT YOUR FEET, LEAVING YOUR LEG OUT JUST ENOUGH TO TRIP HIM INTO THE POOL.

OH, YOU'VE REALLY DONE IT NOW, NICK.

GEESH!

ONE DOWN, ONE TO GO

NICK? WHAT ARE YOU DOING? COBY SAYS.

I GOT THIS, YOU SAY.

NOT SURE IF YOU REALLY DO, BUT REALIZING THERE'S NO TURNING BACK NOW.

DEAN'S DOGGY PADDLE(APPARENTLY HE CAN'T SWIM) SENDS EVERYONE INTO A FIT OF RAUCOUS LAUGHTER.

EVERYONE EXCEPT HIS BROTHER, WHO IS NOW WALKING YOUR WAY, LOOKING **MURDEROUS**.

HE'S A FEW FEET AWAY WHEN YOU REALIZE THAT NO DANCE MOVE OR SOCCER TRICK IS GONNA STOP HIS DEATH BLOW.

YOU GLANCE DOWN AT THE LOW TABLE THAT SEPARATES YOU FROM HIS WRATH.

THERE'S A BOOK ON IT:

THE HEROES OF OLYMPUS

IRONIC, YOU THINK.
(FIGHT THE FEAR, NICK.)
(YOU GOT THIS, NICK.)

DON, WAIT A MINUTE. DON'T YOU WANT ONE MORE DAY WITH A CHANCE? YOU ASK, QUOTING MICHONNE OF **THE WALKING DEAD**, BUT WITHOUT A SWORD.

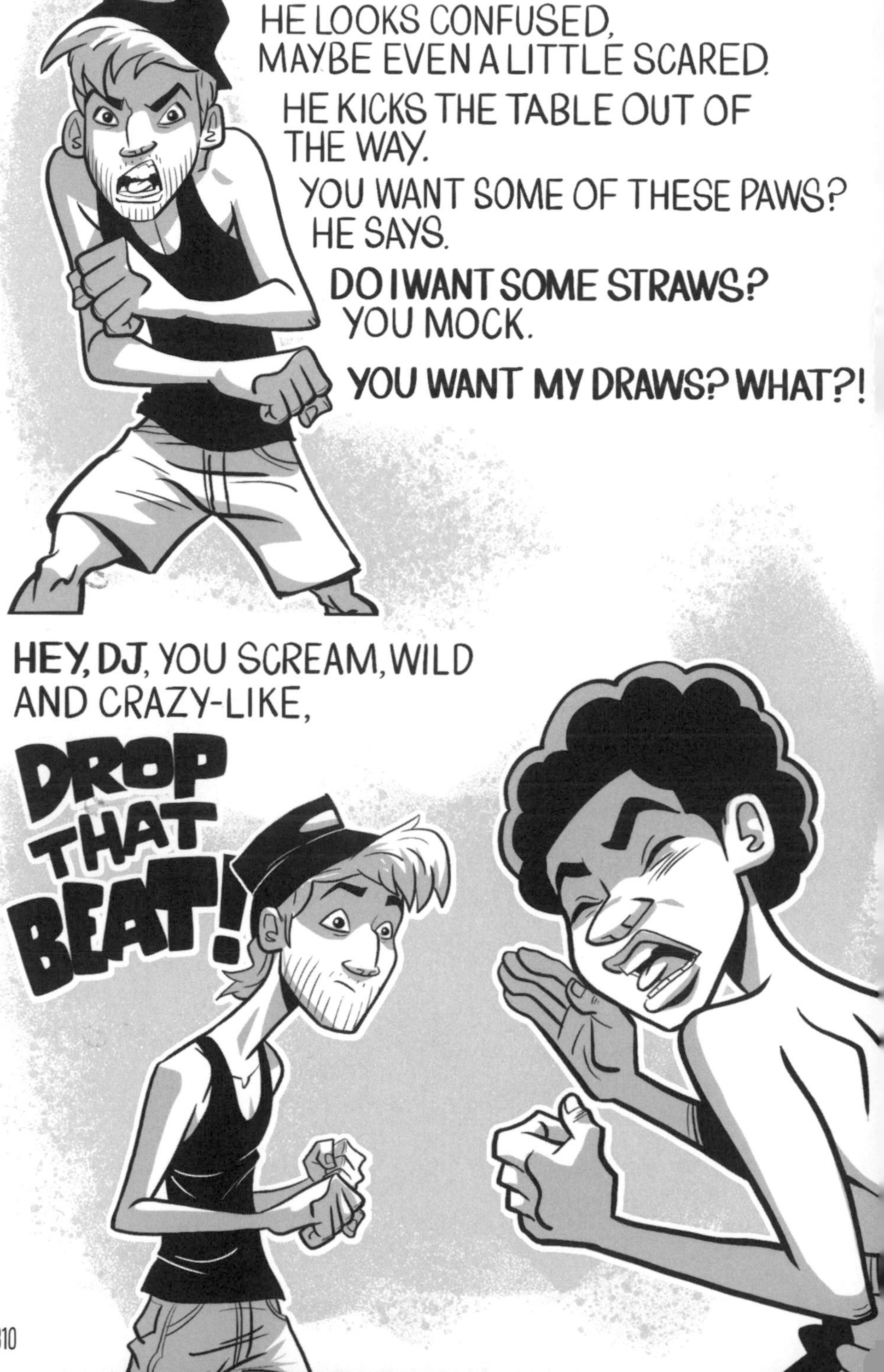
HE LOOKS CONFUSED,
MAYBE EVEN A LITTLE SCARED.
HE KICKS THE TABLE OUT OF
THE WAY.
YOU WANT SOME OF THESE PAWS?
HE SAYS.
DO I WANT SOME STRAWS?
YOU MOCK.
YOU WANT MY DRAWS? WHAT?!
HEY, DJ, YOU SCREAM, WILD
AND CRAZY-LIKE,
DROP THAT BEAT!

AND NOW DON LOOKS REALLY CONFUSED.

THE CROWD STARTS LAUGHING, AND HE THROWS A RIGHT PUNCH AND YOU SUDDENLY REMEMBER HOW TO BLOCK A PUNCH FROM TAE KWON DO.

IT WORKS AND YOU FEEL GOOD, AND FOR ONCE YOU'RE ABOVE WATER.

AND THAT FEELS GREAT TILL A LEFT UPPERCUT POPS UP OUTTA NOWHERE AND YOUR JAW FEELS LIKE IT IS IN YOUR BRAIN AND WAIT, WHO SHUT OFF

ALL.

THE.

LIGHTS.

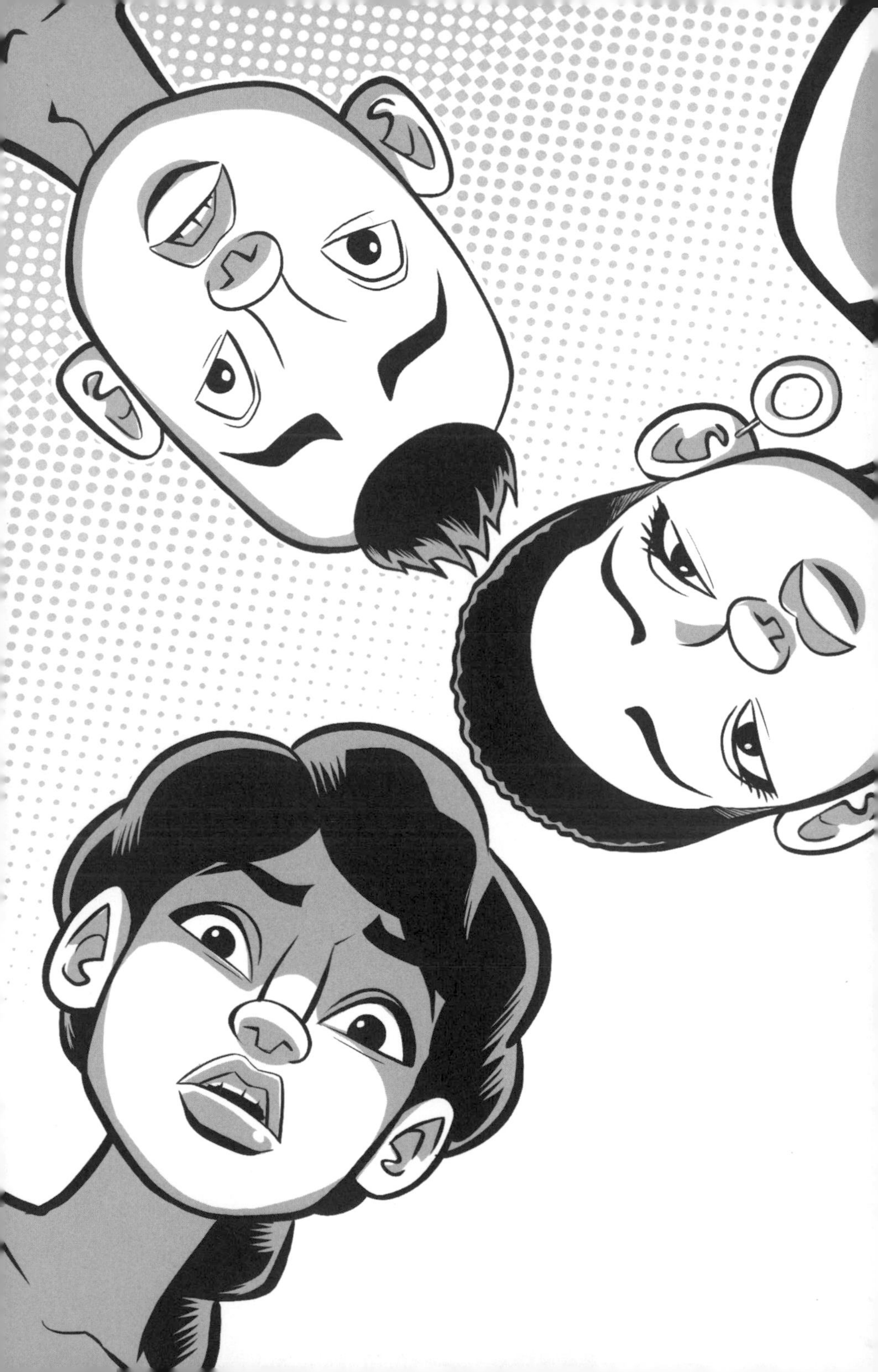

FREEDOM

I THOUGHT YOU WERE DEAD.

DON'T WORRY ABOUT ME, COBY. I KNOW HOW TO TAKE A PUNCH.

YEAH, RIGHT IN THE FACE. YOU WENT DOWN LIKE A MATTRESS. AND THEN YOU HIT YOUR HEAD ON THE TABLE.

THAT HURT.

IT WAS STILL KINDA COOL, THOUGH, THE WAY YOU TOOK DEAN DOWN.

HE OKAY?

YEAH, HE STARTED SCREAMING THAT HE WAS DROWNING, THEN DON GOT HIM OUT AND THEY LEFT.

COOL!

MAYBE THEY'LL LEAVE US ALONE NOW.

IF THEY KNOW WHAT'S BEST FOR THEM, THEY WILL.

WHAT? BALLET?

HEY, IT WORKED, DIDN'T IT?

I GUESS. EITHER THAT OR CHARLENE'S MOTHER THREATENING TO CALL THE POLICE WORKED.

OH, THEY LEFT YOUR BIKE, TOO.

REALLY?

YEP.

HEY, DID APRIL GIVE ME MOUTH-TO-MOUTH RESUSCITATION?

NOPE, BUT WINNIFRED DID.

WHAT?!

JUST KIDDING.

SHE'S GOING TO THE FORMAL DANCE WITH ME.

NO WAY.

YEP.

COOL.

YOU SHOULD ASK CHARLENE, THEN WE CAN DOUBLE DATE.

YEAH, MAYBE! LET'S GET OUTTA HERE.

LET ME SAY GOODBYE TO APRIL FIRST. COME WITH ME.

SERIOUSLY, DUDE.

OH, I ALMOST FORGOT. THE MAC LET ME OPEN HIS DRAGONFLY BOX.

NO FREAKIN' WAY!

YEP.

OH, SNAP!

YOU'LL NEVER BELIEVE WHAT WAS INSIDE...

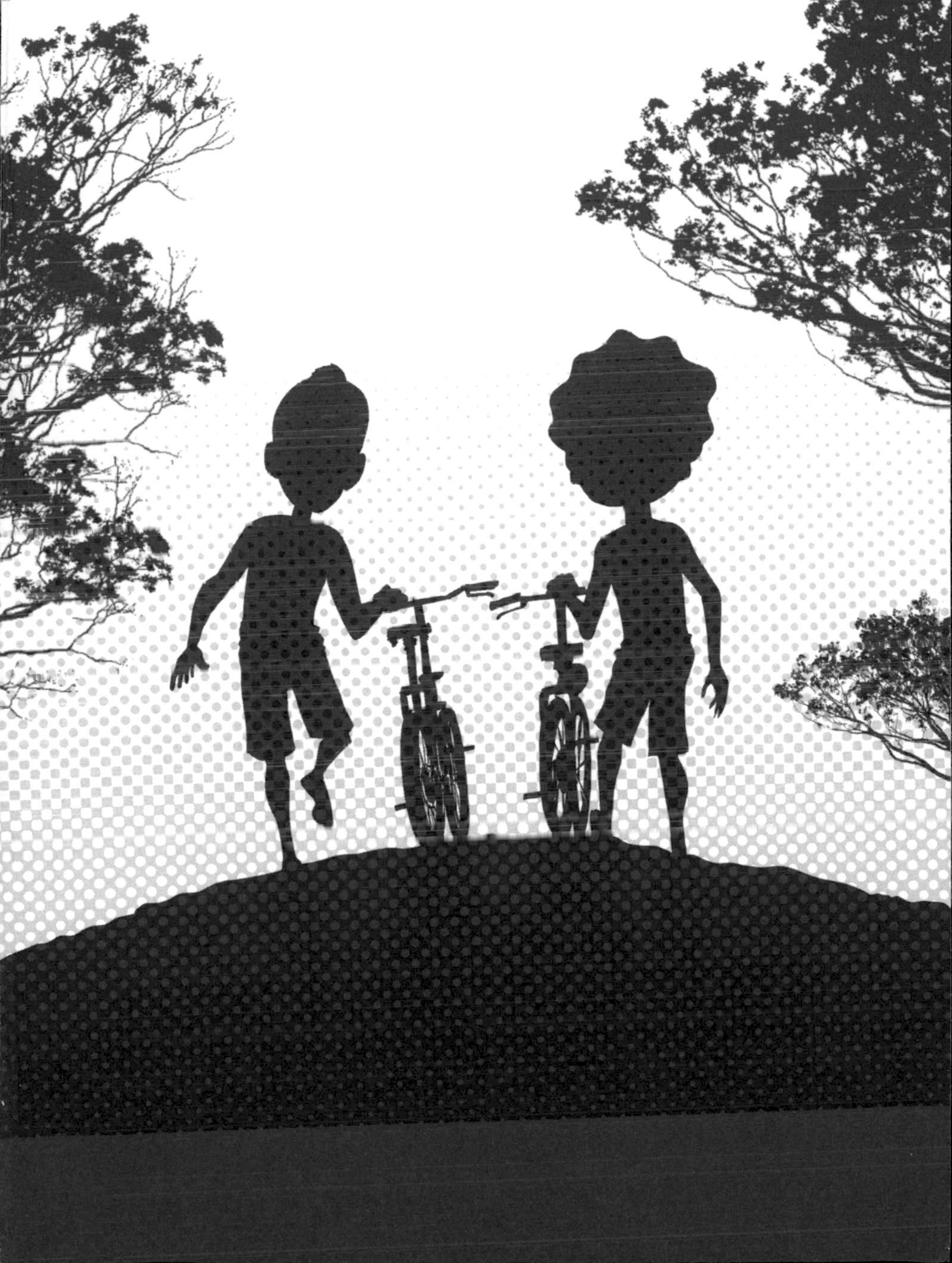

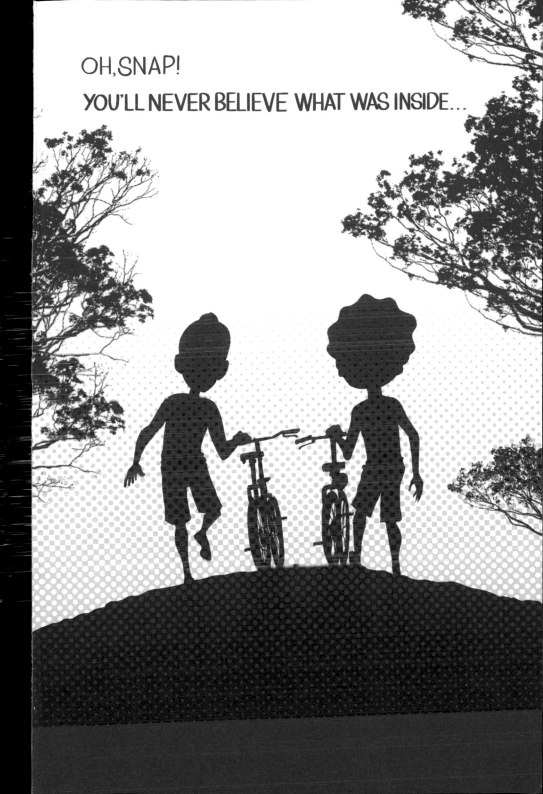